James Campbell was born
contributor to and editor o
Stories. He was editor of th
1978–82, and currently w
Supplement.

The Grafton Book of

Scottish Short Stories

Edited by James Campbell

GRAFTON BOOKS

A Division of the Collins Publishing Group

LONDON GLASGOW
TORONTO SYDNEY AUCKLAND

Grafton Books
A Division of the Collins Publishing Group
8 Grafton Street, London W1X 3LA

Published by Grafton Books 1984
Reprinted 1984, 1986

ISBN 0-586-06165-7

Printed and bound in Great Britain by
Collins, Glasgow

Set in Times

Contents

Preface

James Campbell

In Scotland, talk is often heard of the peculiar strength of the short story. Since all Scots are veterans of the path to delusion signposted 'Wha's like us!' it is as well to step carefully on that ground. Yet it is true to say – even if it is a backhanded compliment – that the Scottish short story has vigour of a kind which the Scottish novel lacks.

It is difficult to say why this should be so. Is the health of short fiction in this century one of the offshoots of a bad crop of longer work in the last? Or is it simply easier to capture the flavour of life on the margins – of politics, of culture, of *England* – which has been the Scots' condition for centuries, in the brief vision which the short story affords? Whichever of these hypotheses is the more plausible, it is a plain fact that writers have made a strength out of weakness, for the short story is treated seriously in Scotland – no writer living there would patronize the form, as an English novelist did recently, as 'chips from a novelist's workbench' – with the result that the contents of this anthology are unusually varied. Deirdre Chapman is in Greece while George Mackay Brown is in Hamnavoe; Alan Spence is rooted in a recognizable reality whereas Alasdair Gray departs from it into fantasy; James Kelman's failure to 'connect' is painfully sad while Brian McCabe's is painfully funny; William Boyd and Giles Gordon are as much at home in Los Angeles and Kashmir as Robin Jenkins is on the golf course. And although it would be largely a wasteful exercise to point glibly to links between the stories or to detect faint traces of national characteristics in them there is one mark which the Scottish writer carries (although he is always at liberty to hide it) which distinguishes him from most European counterparts, and that is a fascination with low life.

Even when national colours are not in evidence – there is nothing at all ostensibly Scottish about William Boyd's 'The Care and Attention of Swimming Pools', for example – the keenness to investigate the dusty corners of other people's lives is present. In the work of Alan Spence, Peter Chaloner, Bernard MacLaverty and Elspeth Davie, to choose some names at random, it is conspicuous.

This is an authentic ingredient in the Scottish personality. In a Scottish village, let's say – the sort of place where it seems possible to get to know everybody – you will find that by far the largest proportion of people are what we call 'ordinary' and, what's more, they expect the people they meet – in this case, you – to be ordinary too. No one would think of saying the same thing about a village in Surrey or Wiltshire.

Perhaps it is this centuries-old experience of plainness which has bestowed on the Scots their most valuable national characteristic, a sense of democracy, which in turn makes Scottish writers aware that although their rightful place is at the world's keyhole, along with Joyce, with Chekhov, with Hemingway, some extra attention should be paid by them to the sights and sounds and smells of the kitchen.

The sixteen stories which follow are drawn from the annual anthology, *Scottish Short Stories*, published by Collins in conjunction with the Scottish Arts Council, the first of which appeared in 1973. Many of these authors had their first publication outside the pages of a little magazine in *Scottish Short Stories*, and several of them have since put out full collections of their own, while there are others on the point of doing so. There are of course some writers included here-whose success was reached by an entirely different route, and yet others who began their careers long before the annual series was conceived, but who have still regarded it, in the past decade or so, as the likeliest occasion to publish new work; writers like George Mackay Brown, Robin Jenkins, Elspeth Davie and Iain Crichton Smith – all represented here – have appeared in *Scottish Short Stories* regularly. In short, there are many expert practitioners of the genre who were born or are presently living in Scotland, and over the past eleven years almost all of them have at some time contributed to the series and have made it what it is.

In the introductory remarks to a recent anthology of classic Scottish short stories, the editor mentioned the names of some living writers whom he admired but had decided to exclude from his book on the quite reasonable grounds that 'they deserve a collection to themselves'. And no doubt – he perhaps meant to add – they will soon be getting one. While it would be misleading to suggest that this collection sets out to represent living Scottish writers comprehensively, many of those whom that editor referred to, by name or implication, are here.

Tithonus:
Fragments from the Diary of a Laird

George Mackay Brown

They are all, especially the women, excited in Torsay to-
day. There is a new child in the village, a little girl. The
birth has happened in a house where – so Traill the
postman assured me – no one for the past ten years has
expected it. The door of Maurice Garth the fisherman and
his wife Armingert had seemed to be marked with the sign
of barrenness. They were married twenty-one years ago,
when Maurice was thirty and Armingert nineteen. One
might have expected a large family, five or six at least,
from such a healthy devoted pair. (They had both come
from tumultuous households to the cold empty cottage at
the end of the village.) But the years passed and no young
voice broke the quiet dialogue of Maurice and Armingert.
To all the islanders it seemed a pity: nothing but beautiful
children could have come from their loins.

I was hauling my dinghy up the loch shore this afternoon – it was too bright a day, the trout saw through every
gesture and feint – when I saw the woman on the road
above. It seemed to me then that she had been waiting to
speak to me for some time. I knew who she must be as
soon as she opened her mouth. The butterings of her
tongue, and the sudden knife flashes, had been described
to me often enough. She was Maggie Swintoun. I had
been well warned about her by the factor and the minister
and the postman. Her idle and wayward tongue, they
told me, had done harm to the reputation of more than
one person in Torsay; so I'm sure that when I turned my

loch-dazzled face to her it did not wear a welcoming expression.

'O sir, you'll never guess,' she said, in the rapt secret voice of all news bearers. 'A bairn was born in the village this morning, and at the Garth cottage of all places – a girl. I think it's right that you should know. Dr Wayne from Hamnavoe took it into the world. I was there helping. I could hardly believe it when they sent for me.'

The face was withdrawn from the loch-side. A rare morning was in front of her, telling the news in shop, smithy, manse and at the doors of all the crofts round about.

I mounted my horse that, patient beast, had been cropping the thin loch-side grass all morning and cantered back to The Hall over the stony dusty road.

Now I knew why a light had been burning at two o'clock in the cottage at the end of the village. I had got up at that time to let Tobias the cat in.

This is the first child to be born in the island since I came to be laird here. I feel that in some way she belongs to me. I stood at the high window of The Hall looking down at the Garth cottage till the light began to fade.

The generations have been renewed. The island is greatly enriched since yesterday.

I suppose that emotionally I am a kind of neutral person, in the sense that I attract neither very much love nor very much dislike. It is eight years since I arrived from London to live in the island that my grand-uncle, the laird of Torsay, a man I had never seen in my life, left to me. On the slope behind the village with its pier and shop and church is The Hall – the laird's residence – that was built in the late seventeenth century, a large elegant house with eighteen rooms, and a garden, and a stable. I am on speaking terms with everyone in the village and with most of the farmers and crofters in the hinterland. Certain people – William Copinsay the shopkeeper, Maggie Swintoun, Grossiter from the farm of Wear – I pass with as curt a nod as I can manage. If I do have a friend, I suppose he must be James MacIntosh who came to be the schoolmaster in the village two summers ago. We play chess in the schoolhouse every Friday night, summer and winter. Occasionally, when he is out walking with his dog, he calls at my place and we drink whatever is in the whisky decanter. (But I insist that his dog, a furtive collie called Joe who occasionally bares his teeth at passers-by, is not let farther than the kitchen – Tobias must not be annoyed.) MacIntosh comes from Perth. He is a pleasant enough man. I think his chief interest is politics, but I do nothing to encourage him when he starts about the Irish question, or the Liberal schism, or the suffragettes, or what the Japanese can be expected to do in such and such an eventuality. I am sure, if I let him go on, that some fine evening he will declare himself to be a socialist. I set the ale-jug squarely between us whenever I hear the first opinionated murmurings; in those malty depths, and there alone, will any argument be.

I think MacIntosh is quite happy living in this island. He is too lazy and too good-natured to be hustled about in a big city school. It is almost certain that he has no real vocation for his job. He has gone to the university, and taken an arts degree, and then enrolled in teaching for want of anything better. But perhaps I do him wrong; perhaps he is dedicated after all to make 'clever de'ils' of the Torsay children. At any rate, the parents and the minister – our education committee representative – seem to have no objection to him. My reason for thinking that he is without taste or talent for the classroom is that he never mentions his work to me; but there again it could simply be, as with politics, that he receives no encouragement.

There is a curious shifting relationship between us, sometimes cordial, sometimes veiled and hostile. He becomes aware from time to time of the social gulf between us, and it is on these occasions that he says and does things to humble me – I must learn that we are living now in the age of equality. But under it all he is such a good-natured chap; after ten minutes or so of unbated tongues we are at peace again over chess-board or decanter.

Last night MacIntosh said, between two bouts of chess in the schoolhouse, 'It's a very strange thing, I did not think I could ever be so intrigued by a child. Most of them are formed of the common clay after all. Oh, you know what I mean – from time to time a beautiful child, or a clever child, comes to the school, and you teach him or her for a year or two, then away they go to the big school in the town, or back to work on the farm, and you never think more about them. But this pupil is just that wee bit different.'

'What on earth are you talking about?' I said.

'The Garth girl who lives at the end of the village – Thora – you know, her father has the fishing boat *Rain Goose*.'

'Is that her name, Thora?' I said. (For I had seen the quiet face among a drift of schoolchildren in the playground, at four o'clock, going home then alone to Maurice's and Armingert's door. I had seen bright hair at the end of the small stone pier, waiting for a boat to come in from the west. I had seen the solemn clasped hands, bearing the small bible, outside the kirk door on a Sunday morning. But beyond that the girl and I had never exchanged a single word. As I say, I did not even know her name till last night.)

'She is a very strange girl, that one,' said MacIntosh. 'There is a *something* about her. Would you please not drop your ash on the mat? (There's an ash-tray.) I'm not like some folk. I can't afford to buy a new mat every month. Mrs Baillie asked me to mention it to you.'

My pipe and his dog cancel each other out. Mrs Baillie is his housekeeper.

'To me she looks an ordinary enough child,' I said. 'In what way is she different?'

MacIntosh could not say how this girl was different. She was made of the common clay – 'like all of us, like all of us,' he hastened to assure me, thereby putting all the islanders, including the laird and Halcro the beachcomber, on the same footing. Still, there was something special about the girl, he insisted, goodness knows what . . .

MacIntosh won the third hard-fought game. He exulted. Victory always makes him reckless and generous. 'Smoke, man, smoke in here any time you like. To hell with Mrs Baillie. Get your pipe out. I'll sweep any ash up myself.'

I met Thora Garth on the brae outside the kirk as I was going home from the schoolhouse. She put on me a brief pellucid unsmiling look as we passed. She was carrying a pail of milk from the farm of Gardyke.

Fifteen years ago, in my grand-uncle's day, the island women stopped and curtsied whenever the laird went past. A century ago a single glance from the great man of The Hall turned them to stone in their fields.

All that is changed.

Traill the postman had put a letter through my window while I was at the schoolhouse. The familiar official writing was on the envelope. I lit the lamp. I was secure in my island for another six months. The usual hundred pounds was enclosed, in a mixture of tens and fives and singles. There was no message; there was usually no need for the Edinburgh lawyer to have anything special to say. He had simply to disburse in two instalments the two hundred pounds a year that my grand-uncle left me, so that I can live out my life as a gentleman in the great Hall of Torsay.

Thora Garth returned this morning from the senior school in Hamnavoe, at the end of her first session there. I happened to be down at the pier when the weekly mail steamer drew alongside. Several islanders were there, as always on that important occasion. The rope came snaking ashore. A seaman shouted banter to the fishermen and Robbie Tenston the farmer of Dale (who had just come out of the hotel bar). The minister turned away, pretending not to have heard the swear-words. I found Maurice Garth standing beside me. 'What's wrong with the creels to-day?' I said to him . . . 'I'm expecting Thora,' Maurice said in that mild shy murmur that many of the islanders have. 'She should be on the boat. It's the summer holidays – she'll be home for seven weeks.'

Sure enough, there was the tilted serious freckled face above the rail. She acknowledged her father with a slight sideways movement of her hand. At that moment I was distracted by an argument that had broken out on the pier. Robbie Tenston of Dale was claiming possession of a large square plywood box that had just been swung ashore from the *Pomona*.

'Nonsense,' cried William Copinsay the general merchant. 'Don't be foolish. It's loaves. It's the bread I always get from the baker in the town on a Friday.'

And indeed – though I hated to agree with Copinsay – there was no doubt that the box contained bread; the incense of new baking drifted across the pier.

'Don't call me a fool,' said Robbie Tenston in his dark dangerous drinking voice. 'This is a box of plants, if you want to know. It's for my wife's greenhouse. The market gardener wrote to say that it was coming on the boat to-day. That's why I'm here, man. Let go of it now.'

Copinsay and Robbie Tenston had each laid hands on the rope that was round the box. A circle of onlookers gathered raggedly about them.

The trouble was, the label had somehow got scraped off in transit. (But Robbie must have been stupid to have missed that delicious smell of new rolls and loaves. Besides, roots and greenery would never have weighed so much.)

They wrestled for the box, both of them red in the face. It had all the makings of a disgraceful scene. Four of the crew had stopped working. They watched from the derrick, delighted. The skipper leaned out of his cabin, grinning eagerly. They could have told who owned the box by rights, but they wanted the entertainment to go on for some time yet.

Mr Evelyn the minister attempted to settle the affair. 'Now now,' he said, 'now now – it is simply a matter of undoing the rope – please, Mr Copinsay – Robert, I beg you – and looking inside.'

They paid no attention to him. The farmer dragged the box from the weaker hands of the merchant. Copinsay's face was twisted with rage and spite. 'You old miserly bastard!' shouted Robbie.

The skipper leaned farther out of his cabin. He put his pipe carefully on the ledge and clapped his hands. Maggie Swintoun and a few other women came down the pier from their houses, attracted by the hullabaloo.

At that point Copinsay flung himself on Robbie Tenston and began to scratch at his face like a woman. He screamed a few falsetto incoherencies.

The dispute had reached a dangerous stage. (I felt that, as the chief man in the island, I should be doing something about it, but I am morbidly afraid of making a fool of myself in front of these people.) Robbie could have taken the merchant in his great earth-red hands and broken him.

He could have picked him up and flung him into the sea. He tried first of all to shake himself free from the hysterical clutchings of William Copinsay. He struck Copinsay an awkward blow on the shoulder. They whirled each other round like mad dancers between the horse box and the gangway. Then – still grappling – they achieved some kind of stillness; through it they glared at each other.

God knows what might have happened then.

It was Thora Garth who restored peace to the island. It was extraordinary, the way the focus shifted from the two buffoons to the girl. But suddenly everyone on the pier, including the skipper and the fighters and myself, was looking at her alone. She had left the steamer and was standing on the pier beside the disputed box. She had one hand on it, laid flat. With the other she pointed to William Copinsay.

'The box belongs to him,' she said quietly. 'Robbie, the box belongs to Mr Copinsay.'

That was the end of the fracas. Robbie Tenston seemed to accept her verdict at once. He pushed Mr Copinsay away. He muttered a grudging 'Well, don't let him or anybody ever call me a fool again.' He walked up the pier, his face encrimsoned, past Maggie Swintoun and the other women who were flocking to the scene, too late, with their false chorus of commiseration and accusation. 'That Robbie Tenston should be reported to the police,' said Maggie Swintoun flatly. 'It's that pub to blame. It should be closed down. Drink is the cause of all the trouble in Torsay. Them in authority should be doing something about it . . .' She kept looking at me out of the corner of her eye.

Mr Copinsay sat on his box of bread and began to weep silently.

I could not bear any more of it.

The seamen had returned to their work, swinging ashore mail bags, crates of beer, saddlery, a bicycle, newspapers. Steve Mack the skipper was lighting his pipe and looking inland to the island hills as if nothing untoward had happened.

I left the women 'cluck-clucking' with sympathy around Copinsay Agonistes. I took my box of books that were sent each month from the library in the town – there was never likely to be any fighting about that piece of cargo – and walked up the pier.

From the gate of The Hall I looked back at the village. Thora Garth was greeting her mother in the open door of their cottage. Maurice carried his daughter's case. The woman and the girl – the one was as tall as the other now – leaned towards each other and kissed briefly. The dog barked and danced around them.

On the top of the island, where the road cuts into the shoulder of the hill, a small dark figure throbbed for a minute against the sky. It was Robbie Tenston bearing his resentment and shame home to Dale.

This evening I called in at the hotel bar for a glass of beer – a thing I rarely do; but it has been, for Orkney, a warm day, and also I must confess I am missing James MacIntosh already – he went home to Perth for the summer vacation two days ago. Seven weeks without chess and argument is a long time.

Maurice Garth was sitting in the window seat drinking stout. I took my glass of beer across to his table.

'Well,' I said, 'and how is Thora liking the big school in Hamnavoe?'

'She isn't clever,' he said, smiling. 'I doubt she won't go very far as a scholar. But what is there for a lass to do in Torsay nowadays? Everybody's leaving the island. I suppose in the end she might get some kind of a job in the town.'

'It was remarkable,' I said, 'the way Thora put a stop to that fight on the pier this morning.'

'Oh, I don't know,' said Maurice. 'That pair of idiots! Any fool could have seen that it was a bread box. I hope we'll hear no more about it. I hope there isn't going to be any trouble about it with the police.'

'They might have done each other an injury,' I said. 'It was your Thora who brought them to their senses. I never saw anything quite so astonishing.'

'No, no,' said Maurice, raising his hand. 'Don't say that. Thora's just an ordinary lass. There's nothing so very strange about it. Thora just pointed out what was what to that pair of fools. Say no more about it.'

Maurice Garth is a placid man. Such vehemence is strange, coming from him. But perhaps it was that he had drunk too many glasses of stout.

There has been a fine morsel of scandal in the village this morning. The Swintoun woman has been going about the doors at all hours, her cheeks aflame with excitement. It seems that the younger son of Wear, the main farm in the island, has been jilted. Everything has been set fair for a wedding for three months past. Consignments of new furniture, carpets, curtains, crockery have been arriving in the steamer from Hamnavoe; to be fetched later the same afternoon by a farm servant in a cart. They do things in style at Wear. The first friends have gone with their gifts, even. I myself wandered about the empty caverns of this house all one morning last week, considering whether this oil painting or that antique vase might be acceptable. The truth is, I can hardly afford any more to give them a present of money. In the end I thought they might be happy with an old silk sampler framed in mahogany that one of my great-aunts made in the middle of Queen Victoria's reign. It is a beautiful piece of work. At Wear they would expect something new and glittery from the laird. I hoped, however, that the bride might be pleased with my present.

The Rev. Mr Evelyn was going to have made the first proclamation from the pulpit next Sunday morning. (I never attend the church services here myself, being nominally an episcopalian, like most of the other Orkney lairds.)

Well, the island won't have to worry any more about this particular ceremony, for – so Traill the postman told me over the garden wall this morning – the prospective bride has gone to live in a wooden shack at the other end of the island – a hut left over from the war – with Shaun Midhouse, a deck-hand on the *Pomona*, a man of no particular comeliness or gifts – in fact, a rather unprepossessing character – certainly not what the women of Torsay would call 'a good catch', by any means.

I am sorry for Jack Grossiter of Wear. He seems a decent enough young chap, not at all like some others in the household. His father of all men I dislike in Torsay. He is arrogant and overbearing towards those whom he considers his inferiors; but you never saw such capraisings and foot-scrapings as when he chances to meet the minister or the schoolmaster or myself on the road. He is also the wealthiest man in the island, yet the good tilth that he works belongs to me, and I am forbidden by law to charge more than a derisory rent for it. I try not to let this curious situation influence me, but of course it does nothing to sweeten my regard for the man. In addition to everything else he is an upstart and an ignoramus. How delighted he was when his only daughter Sophie married that customs house officer two years ago – that was a feather in his cap, for according to the curious snobbery of folk like Grossiter a man who has a pen-and-paper job is a superior animal altogether to a crofter who labours all his

life among earth and blood and dung. The elder son
Andrew will follow him in Wear, no doubt, for since that
piece of socialism was enacted in parliament in 1882 even
death does not break the secure chain of a family's tenure
. . . For Andrew, in his turn, a good match was likewise
negotiated, no less than Mr Copinsay the merchant's
daughter. Wear will be none the poorer for that alliance.
Only Jack Grossiter remained unmarried. Whom he took
to wife was of comparatively small importance – a hill
croft would be found for him when the time came. I could
imagine well enough the brutish reasonings of the man of
Wear, once his second son began to be shaken with the
ruddiness and restlessness of virility. There was now, for
instance, that bonny respectable well-handed lass in the
village – Thora Garth – what objection could there be to
her? She would make a good wife to any man, though of
course her father was only a fisherman and not overbur-
dened with wealth. One afternoon – I can picture it all –
the man of Wear would have said a few words to Maurice
Garth in the pub, and bought him a dram. One evening
soon after that Jack Grossiter and Thora would have been
left alone together in the sea-bright room above the shore;
a first few cold words passed between them. It gradually
became known in the village that they were engaged. I
have seen them, once or twice this summer, walking along
the shore together into the sunset.

Now, suddenly, this has shaken the island.

The first unusual thing to happen was that Thora went
missing, one morning last week. She simply walked out of
the house with never a word to her parents. There had
been no quarrel, so Armingert assured the neighbours.
For the first hour or two she didn't worry about Thora; she
might have walked up to Wear, or called on Minnie
Farquharson who was working on the bridal dress. But
she did not come home for her dinner, and that was

unusual, that was a bit worrying. Armingert called at this door and that in the afternoon. No one had seen Thora since morning. Eventually it was Benny Smith the ferry-man who let out the truth, casually, to Maurice Garth, at the end of the pier, when he got back from Hamnavoe in the early evening. He had taken Thora across in his boat the *Lintie* about ten o'clock that morning. She hadn't said a word to him all the way across. It wasn't any concern of his, and anyway she wasn't the kind of young woman who likes her affairs to be known.

Well, that was a bit of a relief to Maurice and Armingert. They reasoned that Thora must suddenly have thought of some necessary wedding purchase; she would be staying overnight with one of her Hamnavoe friends (one of the girls she had been to school with); she would be back on the *Pomona* the next morning.

And in fact she did come back on Friday on board the *Pomona*. She walked at once from the boat to her parents' door. Who was trailing two paces behind her but Shaun Midhouse, one of the crew of the *Pomona*. Thora opened the cottage door and went inside (Shaun lingered at the gate). She told her mother – Maurice was at the lobsters – that she could not marry Jack Grossiter of Wear after all, because she had discovered that she liked somebody else much better. There was a long silence in the kitchen. Then her mother asked who this other man was. Thora pointed through the window. The deck-hand was shuffling about on the road outside with that hangdog look that he has when he isn't working or drinking. 'That's my man,' Thora said – I'm going to live with him.' Armingert said that she would give much pain and grief to those near to her if she did what she said she was going to do. Thora said she realized that. 'I'm sorry,' she said. Then she left the cottage and walked up the brae to the farm of Wear. Shaun went a few paces with her through the village, but left her outside the hotel and went back on board the *Pomona*; the boat was due to sail again in ten minutes.

Thora wouldn't go into the farmhouse. She said what she had to say standing in the door, and it only lasted a minute. Then she turned and walked slowly across the yard to the road. The old man went a few steps after her, shouting and shaking his fists. His elder son Andrew called him back, coldly – his father mustn't make a fool of himself before the whole district. Let the slut go. His father must remember that he was the most important farmer in Torsay.

Jack had already taken his white face from the door – it hasn't been seen anywhere in the island since. I am deeply sorry for him.

I ought to go along and see these people. God knows what I can say to them. I am hopeless in such situations. I was not created to be a bringer of salves and oils.

I saw the minister coming out of the farmhouse two days ago . . .

The eastern part of the island is very desolate, scarred with peatbogs and Pictish burial places. During the war the army built an artillery battery on the links there. (They commandeered the site – my subsequent granting of permission was an empty token.) All that is left of the camp now, among concrete foundations, is a single wooden hut that had been the officers' mess. No one has lived there since 1919 – inside it must be all dampness and mildew. Tom Christianson the shepherd saw, two days after the breaking of the engagement, smoke coming from the chimney of the hut. He kept an eye on the place; later that afternoon a van drove up; Shaun Midhouse carried from van to hut a mattress, a sack of coal, a box of groceries. He reported the facts to me. That night, late, I walked between the hills and saw a single lamp burning in the window.

Thora Garth and Shaun Midhouse have been living there for a full week now – as Mr Copinsay the merchant says, 'in sin'; managing to look as he says it both pained and pleased.

Two nights ago Armingert and Maurice came to see me.

'Shaun Midhouse is such a poor weed of a creature,' said Armingert in my cold library. 'What ever could any girl see in the likes of *that*?'

Maurice shook his head. They are, both these dear folk, very troubled.

'Jack Grossiter is ill,' said Armingert. 'I never saw a boy so upset. I am very very sorry for him.'

'I will go and see him tomorrow,' I said.

'What trouble she has caused,' said Armingert. 'I did not think such a thing was possible. If she had suddenly attacked us with a knife it would have been easier to bear. She is a bad cruel deceptive girl.'

'She is our daughter,' said Maurice gently.

'We gave no business to inflict our troubles on you,' said Armingert. 'What we have come about is this, all the same. We understand that you own that war-time site. They are sitting unbidden in your property, Thora and that creature. That is what it amounts to. You could evict them.'

I shook my head.

'You could have the law on them,' she insisted. 'You could force them out. She would have to come home then, if you did that. That would bring her to her senses.'

'I'm sorry,' I said. 'There is something at work here that none of us understands. I am not wise enough to interfere.'

There was silence in the library for a long time after that.

Armingert looked hurt and lost. No doubt she is offended with me.

'He is right,' said Maurice at last. 'She is our daughter. We must just try to be patient.'

Then they both got to their feet. They looked tired and sad. They who had been childless for so long in their youth are now childless again; and they are growing old; and an area of their life where there was nothingness twenty years ago is now all vivid pain.

I knew it would happen some day: that old schoolhouse dog has savaged one of the islanders, and a child at that. I was in the garden, filling a bowl with gooseberries, when I heard the terrible outcry from the village, a mingling of snarls and screams. 'Joe, you brute!' came James Mac-Intosh's voice (it was a still summer evening; every sound carried for miles) – 'Bad dog! Get into the house this minute!' . . . And then in a soothing voice, 'Let's see your leg then. It's only a graze, Mansie. You got a fright, that's all . . . That bad Joe . . . Shush now, no need to kick up such a row. You'll deafen the whole village . . .' This Mansie, whoever he was, refused to be comforted. The lamentation came nearer. I heard the schoolhouse door being banged shut (my garden wall is too high to see the village): James MacIntosh had gone indoors, possibly to chastise his cur. Presently a boy, sobbing and snivelling in spasms, appeared on the road. He leaned against a pillar to get his breath. 'Hallo,' I said, 'would you like some gooseberries?'

Greed and self-pity contended in Mansie's face. He unlatched the gate and came in, limping. There was a livid crescent mark below his knee. He picked a fat gooseberry from my bowl. He looked at it wonderingly. His lips were still shivering with shock.

'That damn fool of a dog,' I said. 'Did he seize you then! You better come into the kitchen. I'll put some disinfectant on it. I have bandages.'

The cupped palm of his hand brimmed with gooseberries. He bit into several, one after the other, with a half-reluctant lingering relish. Then he crammed six or seven into his mouth till his cheek bulged. His brown eyes dissolved in rapture; he closed them; there was a runnel of juice from one corner of his mouth to his chin.

The day was ending in a riot of colour westward. Crimson and saffron and jet the sea blazed, like stained glass.

'The disinfectant,' I said. 'It's in the kitchen.'

He balanced the last of the gooseberries on the tip of his tongue, rolling it round inside his mouth, and bit on it. 'It's nothing,' he said. 'I was in the village visiting my grand-da. It was me to blame really. I kicked Joe's bone at the school gate. I must be getting home now. Thora'll be wondering about me . . .'

So, he was one of the Midhouse boys. He looked like neither of his parents. He had the shy swift gentle eyes of Maurice his grandfather. He relished gooseberries the way that old Maurice sipped his stout in the hotel bar.

'And anyway,' he said, 'I wouldn't come into your house to save my life.'

'What's wrong with my house?' I said.

'It's the laird's house,' he said. 'It's The Hall. I'm against all that kind of thing. I'm a communist.' (He was maybe ten years old.)

'There isn't anything very grand about this great ruckle of stones,' I said. 'It's falling to pieces. You should see the inside of it. Just look at this wilderness of a garden. I'll tell you the truth, Mansie – I'm nearly as poor as Ezra the tinker. So come in till I fix your leg.'

He shook his head. 'It's the principle of it,' said Mansie. 'You oppressed my ancestors. You taxed them to death. You drove them to Canada and New Zealand. You made them work in your fields for nothing. They built this house for you, yes, and their hands were red carrying up stones from the shore. I wouldn't go through your door for a pension. What does one man want with a big house like this anyway? Thora and me and my brothers live in two small rooms up at Solsetter.'

'I'm sorry, Mansie,' I said. 'I promise I won't ever be wicked like that again. But I am worried about that bite on your leg.'

'It's the same with the kirk,' said Mansie. 'Do you think I could just have one more gooseberry? I would never enter that kirk door. All that talk about sin and hell and angels. Do you know what I think about the Bible? It's one long fairy-tale from beginning to end. I'm an atheist, too. You can tell the minister what I said if you like. I don't care. I don't care for any of you.'

The rich evening light smote the west gable of The Hall. The great house took, briefly, a splendour. The wall flushed and darkened. Then with all its withered stonework and ramshackle rooms it began to enter the night.

The gooseberry bush twanged. The young anarchist was plucking another fruit.

'I don't believe in anything,' he said. 'Nothing at all. You are born. You live for a while. Then you die. My grandma died last year. Do you know what she is now? Dust in the kirkyard. They could have put her in a ditch, it would have been all the same. When you're dead you're dead.'

'You'd better be getting home then, comrade, before it's dark,' I said.

'Do you know this,' he said, 'I have no father. At least, I do have a father but he doesn't live with us any more. He went away one day, suddenly. Oh, a while ago now, last winter. Jock Ritch saw him once in Falmouth. He was on a trawler. We don't know where he is. I'm glad he's gone. I didn't like him. And I'll tell you another thing.'

'To-morrow,' I said. 'You must go home now. You must

get that bite seen to. If you don't, some day there'll be an old man hobbling round this village with a wooden leg. And it'll be you, if you don't show that wound to your mother right away.'

'Rob and Willie and me,' he said, 'we're bastards. I bet I've shocked you. I bet you think I said a bad word. You see, Thora was never married. Thora, she's my mother. I suppose you would say "illegitimate" but it's just the same thing. The gooseberries were good. They're not your gooseberries though. They belong to the whole island by rights. I was only taking my share.'

The darkness had come down so suddenly that I could not say when the boy left my door. I was aware only that one smell had been subtracted from the enchanting cluster of smells that gather about an island on a late summer evening. A shadow was gone from the garden. I turned and went inside, carrying the bowl of gooseberries. (There would be one pot of jam less next winter.) I traversed, going to the kitchen, a corridor with an ancient ineradicable sweetness of rot in it.

I have been ill, it seems. I feel like a ghost in a prison of bone. I have been very ill, James MacIntosh says. 'I thought you were for the kirkyard,' he told me last night. 'That's the truth. I thought an ancient proud island family was guttering out at last . . .' He said after a time, 'There's something tough about you, man. I think you'll see the boots off us all.' He put the kettle on my fire to make a pot of tea. 'I don't suppose now,' he said, 'that you'll be up to a game of chess just yet. Quite so.' He is a sweet considerate man. 'I'll fill your hot-water bottle before I go,' he said, 'it's very cold up in that bedroom.'

The whole house is like a winter labyrinth in the heart of this summer-time island. It is all this dampness and rot, I'm sure, that made me so ill last month. The Hall is withering slowly about me. I cannot afford now to re-slate the roof. There is warping and woodworm and patches of damp everywhere. The three long corridors empty their overplus of draughts into every mildewed bedroom. Even last October, when the men from the fishing boat broke the billiard-room window, going between the hotel and the barn dance at Dale, I had to go without tobacco for a fortnight or so until the joiner was paid. Not much can be done these days on two hundred pounds a year.

'James,' I said, 'I'm going to shift out of that bedroom. Another winter there and I'd be a goner. I wonder if I could get a small bed fitted into some corner of the kitchen – over there, for example, out of the draught. I don't mind eating and sleeping in the same room.'

This morning (Saturday) MacIntosh came up from the schoolhouse with a small iron folding bed. 'It's been in the outhouse since I came to Torsay,' he said. 'The last teacher must have had it for one of his kids. It's a bit rusty, man, but it's sound, perfectly sound. Look for yourself. If you'll just shift that heap of books out of the corner I'll get it fixed up in no time . . .'

We drank some tea while blankets and pillows were airing at the kitchen fire. I tried to smoke my pipe but the thing tasted foul – the room plunged; there was a blackness before my eyes; I began to sweat. 'You're not entire well yet by any means,' said the schoolmaster. 'Put that pipe away. It'll be a week or two before you can get over the door, far less down to the hotel for a pint. I'm telling you, you've been very ill. You don't seem to realize how desperate it was with you. But for one thing only you'd be in the family vault.'

People who have been in the darkness for a while long to know how it was with them when they were no longer there to observe and evaluate. They resent their absence from the dear ecstatic flesh; they suspect too that they may have been caught out by their attendants in some weakness or shame that they themselves make light of, or even indulge, in the ordinary round. At the same time there is a kind of vanity in sickness. It sets a person apart from the folk who only eat and sleep and sorrow and work. Those dullards become the servants of the hero who has ventured into the shadowy border-land next to the kingdom of death – the sickness bestows a special quality on him, a seal of gentility almost. There are people who wear their scars and pock-marks like decorations. The biography of such a one is a pattern of small sicknesses, until at last the kingdom he has fought against and been fascinated with for so long besets him with irresistible steel and fire. There is one last trumpet call under a dark tower . . .

This afternoon, by means of subtle insistent questions, I got from James MacIntosh the story of my trouble. He would much rather have been sitting with me in amiable silence over a chess-board. I knew of course the beginning of the story; how I had had to drag myself about the house for some days at the end of May with a grey quake on me. To get potatoes from the garden – a simple job like that – was a burdensome penance. The road to the village and the tobacco jar on Mr Copinsay's shelf was a wearisome *via crucis*, but at last I could not even get that far. My pipe lay cold on the window-sill for two days. Some time during the third day the sun became a blackness.

'Pneumonia,' said James MacIntosh. 'That's what it was. Dr Wayne stood in the schoolhouse door and barked at me. *The laird up yonder, your friend, he has double pneumonia. By rights he should be ferried to the hospital in Kirkwall. That's out of the question, he's too ill. He'll have to bide where he is . . . Now then* (says he) *there's not a hell of a lot I can do for him. That's the truth. It's a dicey thing, pneumonia. It comes to a crisis. The sick man reaches a*

*cross-roads, if you understand what I mean. He lingers
there for an hour or two. Then he simply goes one way or
the other. There's no telling. What is essential though* (says
the old quack) *is good nursing. There must be somebody
with him night and day – two, if possible, one to relieve the
other. Now then, you must know some woman or other in
the island who has experience of this kind of thing. Get her*
. . . And out of the house he stumps with his black bag,
down the road, back to the ferry-boat at the pier.

'So there you lay, in that great carved mahogany bed
upstairs, sweating and raving. Old Wayne had laid the
responsibility fairly and squarely on me. I had to get a
nurse. But what nurse? And where? The only person who
does any kind of nursing in the island is that Maggie
Swintoun – at least, she brings most of the island bairns
into the world, and it's her they generally send for when
anybody dies. But nursing – I never actually heard of her
attending sick folk. And besides, I knew you disliked the
woman. If you were to open your eyes and see that face at
the foot of the bed it would most likely, I thought, be the
end of you. But that didn't prevent Mistress Swintoun
from offering her services that same day. There she stood,
keening and whispering at the foot of the stair – she had
even had the impudence to come in without knocking. *I
hear the laird isn't well, the poor man* (says she).*Well now,
if there's anything I can do. I don't mind sitting up all night*
. . . And the eyes of her going here and there over the
portraits in the staircase and over all the silver plate in the
hall-stand. *Thank you all the same*, said I, *but other
arrangements have been made* . . . Off she went then like a
cat leaving a fish on a doorstep. I was worried all the
same, I can tell you. I went down to the village to have a
consultation with Minnie Farquhar the seamstress. She
knows everybody in Torsay, what they can do and what
they can't do. She demurred. In the old days there would

have been no difficulty: the island was teeming with kindly capable women who would have been ideal for the job. But things are different now, Minnie pointed out. Torsay is half empty. Most of the houses are in ruin. The young women are away in the towns, working in shops and offices. All that's left in the way of women-folk are school bairns and "puir aald bodies". She honestly couldn't think of a single suitable person. *Now* (says she) *I doubt you'll have to put an advertisement in* The Orcadian.

'I knew, as I walked back up the brae, that by the time the advertisement – "Wanted, experienced private nurse to attend gentleman" – had appeared and been answered, and the nurse interviewed and approved and brought over to Torsay, there would have been no patient for her to attend to. The marble jaws would have swallowed you up . . .

'When I turned in at the gate of The Hall, I saw washed sheets and pillow-cases hanging in the garden, between the potato patch and the gooseberry bushes, where no washing has ever flapped in the wind for ten years and more. (You hang your shirts and socks, I know, in front of the stove.) I went into the house. The fire was lit in the kitchen. The windows along the corridor were open, and there was a clean sweet air everywhere instead of those grey draughts. I'm not a superstitious man, but I swear my hand was shaking when I opened the door of your bedroom. And there she was, bent over you and putting cold linen to the beaded agony on your face.'

'Who?' I said.

'And there she stayed for ten days, feeding you, washing you, comforting you, keeping the glim of life in you night and day. Nobody ever relieved her. God knows when she slept. She was never, as far as I could make out, a minute away from your room. But of course she must have been, to cook, wash, prepare the medicines, things like that. She had even set jars of flowers in odd niches and corners. The house began to smell fragrant.'

I said, 'Yes, but who?'

'She told me, standing there in your bedroom that first day, that I didn't need to worry any longer. She thought she could manage. What could I do anyway, she said, with the school bairns to teach from ten in the morning till four in the afternoon? And she smiled at me, as though there was some kind of conspiracy between us. And she nodded, half in dismissal and half in affirmation. I went down that road to the schoolhouse with a burden lifted from me, I can tell you. *Well, if he doesn't get better*, I thought, *it won't be for want of a good nurse.*'

'You haven't told me her name,' I said.

'On the Thursday old Wayne came out of The Hall shaking his head. I saw him from the school window. He was still shaking his head when he stepped on board the *Lintie* at the pier. That was the day of the crisis. I ran up to your house as soon as the school was let out at half past three (for I couldn't bear to wait till four o'clock). The flame was gulping in the lamp all right. Your pulse had no cohesion or rhythm. There were great gaps in your breathing. I stood there, expecting darkness and silence pretty soon. What is it above all that a woman gives to a man? God knows. Some strong pure dark essence of the earth that seems not to be a part of the sun-loving clay of men at all. The woman was never away from your bedside that night. I slept, on and off, between two chairs in the kitchen. At sunrise next morning you spoke for the first time for, I think, twelve days. You asked for – of all things – a cup of tea. But the nurse, she was no longer there.'

'For God's sake,' I said, 'tell me who she is.'

'You'll have to be doing with my crude services,' said James MacIntosh, 'till you're able to do for yourself.

You should be out and about in a week, if this good weather holds. I thought I told you who she was.'

'You didn't,' I said.

'Well now,' he said, 'I thought I did. It was Thora Garth, of course.'

This morning I had a visit from a young man I have never seen before. It turns out that he is a missionary, a kind of lay Presbyterian preacher. There has been no minister in Torsay since the Rev. Mr Evelyn retired three years ago; the spiritual needs of the few people remaining have been attended to, now and then, by ministers from other islands.

This missionary is an earnest young bachelor. He has a sense of vocation but no humour. Someone in the village must have told him about me. 'Mister, you'd better call on the old man up at The Hall. You'll likely be able to understand the posh way he speaks. He only manages down to the village once a week nowadays for his tobacco and his margarine and his loaf. He has nothing to live on but an annuity – nowadays, with the price of things, it would hardly keep a cat. The likes of him is too grand of course to apply for Social Security. God knows what way he manages to live at all. He's never been a church man, but I'm sure he'd be pleased to see an educated person like you . . .' I can just imagine Andrew Grossiter, or one of the other elders, saying that to the newcomer some Sunday morning after the service, pointing up the brae to the big house with the fallen slates and the broken sundial.

So, here he was, this young preacher, come to visit me out of Christian duty. He puts on me a bright kind smile from time to time.

'I like it here, in Torsay,' he said. 'Indeed I do. It's a great change from the city. I expect it'll take me a wee while to get used to country ways. I come from Glasgow myself. For example, I'm as certain as can be that someone has died in the village this morning. I saw a man carrying trestles into one of the houses. There was a coffin in the back of his van. By rights I should have been told about it at once. It's my duty to visit the bereaved relatives. I'll be wanted of course for the funeral. Ah well, I'll make enquiries this afternoon some time.'

He eyed with a kind of innocent distaste the sole habitable room left in my house, the kitchen. If I had known he was coming I might have tidied the place up a bit. But for the sake of truth it's best when visitors come unexpectedly on the loaf and cracked mug on the table, the unmade bed, the webbed windows, and all the mingled smells of aged bachelordom.

'Death is a common thing in Torsay nowadays,' I said. 'Nearly everybody left in the village is old. There's hardly a young person in the whole island except yourself.'

'I hope you don't mind my visiting you,' said the missionary. 'I understand you're an episcopalian. These days we must try to be as ecumenical as we can. Now sir, please don't be offended at what I'm going to say. It could be that, what with old age and the fact that you're not so able as you used to be, you find yourself with less money than you could be doing with – for example, to buy a bag of coal or a bit of butcher-meat.'

'I manage quite well,' I said. 'I have an annuity from my grand-uncle. I own this house. I don't eat a great deal.'

'Quite so,' he said. 'But the cost of everything keeps going up. Your income hardly covers the little luxuries that make life a bit more bearable. Now, I've been looking through the local church accounts and I've discovered that there are one or two small bequests that I have the disposal of. I don't see why you shouldn't be a beneficiary. They're for every poor person in the island, whatever church he belongs to, or indeed if he belongs to no church at all.'

'I don't need a thing,' I said.

'Well,' he said, 'if ever you feel like speaking to me about it. The money is there. It's for everybody in Torsay who needs it.'

'Torsay will soon require nothing,' I said.

'I must go down to the village now and see about this death,' he said. 'I noticed three young men in dark suits coming off the *Pomona* this morning. They must be relatives of some kind . . . I'll find my own way out. Don't bother. This is a fascinating old house right enough. These stones, if only they could speak. God bless you, now.'

He left me then, that earnest innocent young man. I was glad in a way to see the back of him – though I liked him well enough – for I was longing for a pipeful of tobacco, and I'm as certain as can be that he is one of those evangelicals who disapprove of smoking and drinking.

So, there is another death in the island. Month by month Torsay is re-entering the eternal loneliness and silence. The old ones die. The young ones go away to farm in other places, or to car factories in Coventry or Bathgate. The fertile end of the island is littered with roofless windowless crofts. Sometimes, on a fine afternoon, I take my stick and walk for an hour about my domain. Last week I passed Dale, which Robbie Tenston used to farm. (He has been in Australia for fifteen years.) I pushed open the warped door of the dwelling-house. A great grey ewe lurched past me out of the darkness and nearly knocked me over. Birds whirred up through the bare rafters. There were bits of furniture here and there – a table, a couple of chairs, a wooden shut-bed. A framed photograph of the Channel Fleet still hung at the damp wall. There were empty bottles and jam jars all over the floor among sheep-turds and bird-splashes . . . Most of the farmhouses in Torsay are like that now.

It is an island dedicated to extinction. I can never

imagine young people coming back to these uncultivated fields and eyeless ruins. Soon now, I know, the place will be finally abandoned to gulls and crows and rabbits. When first I came to Torsay fifty years ago, summoned from Cambridge by my grand-uncle's executor, I could still read the heraldry and the Latin motto over the great Hall door. There is a vague shape on the sandstone lintel now; otherwise it is indecipherable. All that style and history and romance have melted back into the stone.

Life in a flourishing island is a kind of fruitful inter-weaving music of birth and marriage and death: a trio. The old pass mildly into the darkness to make way for their bright grandchildren. There is only one dancer in the island now and he carries the hourglass and the spade and the scythe.

How many have died in the past few years? I cannot remember all the names. The severest loss, as far as I am concerned, is James MacIntosh. The school above the village closed ten years ago, when the dominie retired. There were not enough pupils to justify a new teacher. He did not want to leave Torsay – his whole life was entirely rooted here. He loved the trout fishing, and our chess and few drams twice a week; he liked to follow the careers of his former pupils in every part of the world – he had given so much of his life to them. What did he know of his few remaining relatives in Perthshire? 'Here I am and here I'll bide,' he said to me the day the school closed. I offered him a croft a mile away – Unibreck – that had just been vacated: the young crofter had got a job in an Edinburgh brewery. James MacIntosh lived there for two winters, reading his 'Forward' and working out chess moves from the manual he kept beside his bed . . . One morning Maggie Swintoun put her head in at my kitchen door when I was setting the fire. 'O sir,' she wailed, 'a terrible thing has happened!' Every broken window, every winter cough, every sparrow-fall is stuff of tragedy to Maggie Swintoun. I didn't bother even to look round at the woman – I went on laying a careful stratum of sticks on the crumpled paper. 'Up at Unibreck,' she cried, 'your friend, poor Mr MacIntosh the teacher. I expected it. He hasn't been looking well this past month and more . . .' She must have been put out by the coal-blackened face I turned on her, for she went away without rounding off her knell. I gathered later that the postman, going with a couple of letters to the cottage, had found James MacIntosh cold and silent in his armchair . . . I know he would have liked to be buried in Torsay. Those same relatives that he had had no communication with for a quarter of a century ordered his body to be taken down to Dundee. There he was burned in a crematorium and his dust thrown among alien winds.

Maggie Swintoun herself is a silence about the doors of the village. Her ghost is there, a shivering silence, between the sea and the hill. In no long time now that frail remembered keen will be lost in the greater silence of Torsay.

The shutters have been up for two years in the general store. William Copinsay was summoned by a stroke one winter evening from his money bags. They left him in the kirkyard, with pennies for eyes, to grop his way towards that unbearable treasure that is laid up (some say) for all who have performed decent acts of charity in their lives; the acts themselves, subtleties and shadows and gleams in time being (they say again) but fore-reflections of that hoarded perdurable reality. (I do believe this myself. I believe in the 'twelve winds' of Housman that assemble the stuff of life for a year or two and then disperse it again.) Anyway, William Copinsay is dead.

Grossiter died at the auction mart in Hamnavoe, among the beasts and the whisky-smelling farmers, one Wednesday afternoon last spring.

Of course I know who has died in Torsay to-day. I knew hours before that young missionary opened his mouth. I had seen the lamp burning in a window at the end of the village at two o'clock in the morning.

It is not the old man who has died, either. His death could not have given me this unutterable grief that I felt then, and still feel. The heart of the island has stopped beating. I am the laird of a place that has no substance or meaning any more.

I will go down to the cottage some time to-day. I will knock at the door. I will ask for permission to look into that still face.

The only child I have had has been taken from me; the only woman I could ever have loved; the only dust that I wished my own dust to be mingled with.

But in the fifty years that Thora Garth and I have lived in this island together we have never exchanged one word.

The New Place

Deirdre Chapman

Mrs Paton dabbled her toes in the Aegean and shivered.

The Aegean was tepid, like a big bath, she thought, run off a small immerser. Her shiver was spiritual. This same sea now fingering her ankles, titillating her bunion and shooting cool shafts of pleasure up the pain corridors from her boxy feet, this sea had carried fair Helen and Paris to Troy. Mighty Alexander had crossed it. Ulysses had ploughed his wild furrow through it. Poseidon ruled it.

'Home at last,' said Mrs Paton to herself and blushed.

She really was feeling most odd. The sun was nibbling at the nape of her neck, the rocks bit into her bottom, and the afternoon trembled about her in a way that was hard to contain. Down there her toes swam singly in the thick water, at once captured and liberated, like prawns in aspic.

Nothing else moved but the sunlight on the surface of the bay, lumpy and metallic as crushed kitchen foil right out to the next brown island. Behind her the five concrete stories of the Poseidon Beach Hotel were screened by taller rocks. Stacked parallel and horizontal between their private baths and their sea views, Mr Paton on his twin bed, Bill and Mavis from Beckenham, Kent, Lee and Sharon from Boston, Mass., and the nice German couple snored off moussaka and Greek beer while their swimsuits baked dry for the evening dip. Unobserved, Mrs Paton launched herself into the water.

It came up only as far as her collar bone which, she

thought, touching bottom, was just as well, for she had never learned to swim. She had felt no need standing every summer up to her pale calves in the North Sea, lusting after Europe on the other side.

But now as she spread her arms and trembled on her tiptoes, Earth, Air, Fire and Water competing for her, she awarded the golden apple to Water. 'I am in my element,' she said out loud, and laughed as she blushed.

Her large body floated free of gravity and ached with uplift like a pink satin gas-filled balloon. Her bosom spread itself splendidly beneath the surface, her cleavage a cushioned grotto for tired plankton. She moonwalked away from the rocks and music came on in her head, music for floating to shoeless, braless, corsetless. She recognized it as the lost music of the Greek world, the missing complement to the statues, the temples, the poetry. She tried to sing it in her mournful wobbly contralto but it eluded her.

A purple jellyfish sidled past, heading out to sea. A shoal of tiny nervous fish looked right, looked left, looked right again and streaked away in pursuit. High overhead a grey seabird circled. Why, she thought, that's the first bird I've seen since I came to Greece.

She faced the sun and closed her eyes, and in the orange darkness thought of poor Leto, panting with second stage contractions, combing the Aegean for a place to give birth till Poseidon anchored Delos for her. She herself had had a half-hour journey to hospital on the back seat of a Mini, but there the comparison ended. Leto had produced Apollo and that was worth any amount of suffering, especially after the disappointment of a daughter, even Artemis.

Her own daughter had died within an hour of birth and after all these years the memory still held more guilt than sorrow. Ariadne, she had called her. The midwife had snorted with disapproval, afterwards adjusting her face mask in case a Presbyterian germ flew out and landed on the baby. But Ariadne had been beyond the niceties of sterility. Her husband had been shown in and said 'Ariadne McFarlane Ross, then.' Mrs Paton always remembered that as her daughter's epitaph. They had trundled her back to the ward and, behind the chintz curtains they pulled to exclude grief, blood and private parts, she had wept. But even as she wept a subversive voice was whispering that the death of a weak female child was no tragedy. She should have had a son, a hero, but Mr Paton wasn't up to it.

Zeus had been shifty about his mistresses, a side of him she disapproved of though it was manifestly Greek. He had hidden Leto in the guise of a quail, and turned the passive Io into a cow. But jealous Hera had found and pursued them both, sending a gadfly to harry Io till she plunged into the sea. She herself would have shunned his cowskins and faced Hera woman to woman, not that she approved of easy virtue, but Hera reminded her of some of her more self-righteous friends, preaching at unmarried mothers under the cloak of welfare work and blaming the single woman in any triangle.

'Damn Hera,' she said. 'Damn them all.'

Up above the seabird rocked in a sudden puff of wind.

She remembered Silbury's Soups, but for whom she would not be here to-day, basking and bobbing and meditating. It was hard to feel anything warm and personal for such a large firm, but she owed it to them to try. It was their kindness, together with two packets of their Scotch Broth, two Minestrone, one Spring Vegetable and one Lentil with Ham, plus the six requisites for successful menu planning arranged in the order C E A F B D, and the slogan 'Silbury's Soups are better because you taste each garden-fresh vegetable in every vitamin-rich spoonful' that had brought her on this Holiday of a Lifetime, Fifteen Days for Two on a Greek Island.

On the last posting date she had panicked and would have bought fifty-four more packets had it not been early closing day. Instead she sacrificed an unopened bottle of Mateus Rosé to Apollo by breaking it over the sundial, putting the splinters in the dustbin, and telling Mr Paton when he came back from the Rotary Club it had slipped out of her bad hand while she was dusting the cocktail cabinet.

At sunset, watching the sparrows swoop drunkenly over the lawn, she could have sworn she saw his dear golden face peeking at her out of a pink cloud.

Later when the letter came from Silbury's and Greece was in her grasp, Mr Paton had baulked. He brought out a brochure for the Golf Hotel, Nairn. He said he couldn't stand heat or history. The truth was, he was afraid. In a land where no one recognized his F.P. tie or understood his anecdotes he was as good as naked. She would have been sorry for him if she herself hadn't felt naked and foreign every day of her life.

She had come very near to leaving him over it. She had sat up all that night in her separate bed reading her paperback Odyssey, while he tossed and turned, complained about her bed lamp, tramped ostentatiously to the bathroom, rattled tumbler and sleeping tablets. By dawn she was ready to pack her case and go, well aware that the strength of her Hellenic passion compared with her lack of passion in other directions was as good as adulterous.

But over breakfast she found he had changed. Changed miraculously, while she herself was filled with quiet strength. He submitted to signing his passport application and the purchase of boxer shorts. They were here, together.

'And so they lived happily ever after,' declared Mrs

Paton to the sky, and wondered at the cynicism in her voice.

The swimmy feeling that had driven her into the water had come back. She felt as light-headed as if she had drunk sherry before lunch. Light all over in fact. Her brain was acting quite irresponsibly, slipping away into an irritating state of euphoria instead of coming to grips with her condition. And when she tried to fight it, two syllables, repeated, pulsated somewhere just out of reach. She concentrated hard and caught an echo . . . RE-LAX, RE-LAX or was it LIE BACK, LIE BACK? The water lapping mesmerically in and around her ears whispered the offbeat. RE-re-LAX-lax LIE-lie-BACK-back.

'I *am* lying back,' she said. And so she was. Floating.

Flat on her back she marvelled at her expertise. But when she raised her head she rolled and toppled and broke the spell.

Relax, she told herself sternly, lie back. But it was difficult, heaving and gasping as her lungs fussily rejected the merest teaspoonful of sea water.

Steady and in command again, she took stock. Neither the hotel nor its brown rocks had been on her brief horizon.

She paddled cautiously through a forty-five degree turn, like one-sixteenth of a water lily that had Esther Williams as its pistil. The sun should be a guide but it seemed to be everywhere. She pictured herself a log, hoping that way to reduce sudden movement to a controlled roll. But when she raised her head this time her body separated into disorganized branches.

When she finished choking she had no sense of direction beyond up and down. Her panic was controlled by the need to stay steady, but she no longer flopped trustingly upon a polystyrene sea. The many drops of water temporarily united in supporting her spine were not to be relied on. Before plastic, before cellophane, before glass, density had gone hand in hand with opacity and transparent rightly meant fluid.

Something tickled her toes and brushed past her shoulder. She felt life and movement all about her and remembered the little fishes and the purple jellyfish.

She opened her eyes and saw again the seabird directly overhead, describing hypnotic figures, supporting itself easily on nothing. The thought steadied her.

She supposed the Greek Air Force ran an air-sea rescue service. The water was warm. At five Mr Paton would waken and look for her. But the fear stiffening under the bones of her swimsuit was not to be placated by clock-watching. From the rich store of her imagination she drew out an image and concentrated on it.

Alexander. This water had washed the keel of his ship. Maybe even now it was infinitesimally polluted with – er – pitch? Did they have pitch? Oil? Not mineral oil, of course, filthy stuff of dead seabirds and treble pink stamps. *Olive* oil. Pressed from the fruit and massaged into the hulls of beached ships by lovely laughing girls, the new wood glowing sherry and amber under the oil, the rich fruity smell of it, the silky swish of the girls' hands moving in rhythm over the curved hull . . .

Something familiar in the scene was distorting the picture. Ugh. Babies' bottoms and Olive Oil B.P. were getting in the way. She swallowed a crestful of wave, spluttered, and grappled with her vision control. Alexander. Concentrate on him.

Now Alexander stood alone on the deck of a wide ship, his back to the fiery wake and the setting sun. He yearned towards the East, and Mrs Paton yearned towards Alexander, when, all bright and burnished and beautiful, he turned to profile and urinated over the side. The water around her grew warm and pregnant with portent. How *old* was water? Did it go off? It evaporated, of course, on the surface. Urine, being warm, should rise, but then, presumably being heavier than water, it would sink. But would it be heavier than *salt* water? Really there were times one wished one had paid attention in the physics class. Even if it had evaporated, what went up must come down. But did it come down in the same place? It depended on the winds of course. Ye Gods . . . Alexander's urine could very well have rained on her garden in Portobello. Heavily diluted of course. Really, the thought was intolerable, the precious fluid disseminated amongst her neighbours' rhubarb. Altogether it was much more satisfactory to consider it preserved in the Aegean, and who was to prove otherwise? Let them try and she would confront them with the entire output of the classical heroes, Jason and Theseus and Achilles and Heracles, the sheer quantity of it defying evaporation and scepticism and marking this sea indelibly, for ever, buoyant and bubbling . . . so buoyant and bubbling . . . so wildly bubbling . . .

A slap, very twentieth century, as of wet plastic, caught her between the thighs. Revulsion blacked out her vision. She was struggling in a nightmare sea boiling with snorkels and flippers and shiny skin-diving suits and, between her legs, an inflated plastic duck, lifting her out of the water, her hands clutching, slipping, clasping about the neck of the creature, thick neck, heavy body, heavier than water, but floating. Not floating. Swimming. Muscles at work beneath the skin and blood coursing. Warm blood. Mammals. Suckle their young. Such as, for instance, the whale, the porpoise and the . . .

Mrs Paton drew herself upright and, assuming the pose of Artemis, head back, chest out, allowed the dolphin to carry her to the island.

He was waiting for her on the beach. She recognized

him at once by his improbably erect beard and the thunderbolt on the table in front of him.

He rose to greet her, and she was fleetingly anxious, as if planted without notice in the Buckingham Palace line-up. How did one greet the King of the Gods?

He came closer and put his hands on her wet shoulders. She angled a cheek for a kiss – was it left or right first? – but he was no de Gaulle. He held her away and looked her slowly up and down, her varnished damaged toes, her pink satin one-piece, her shaven underarms, her wet yellow perm . . . could he find beauty in them, or dignity?

Mrs Paton inclined her head regally and was led to the table. She tugged modestly at her swimsuit and sat squelchily on the wooden chair which Zeus held for her. He sat opposite and still he did not speak.

The table was set with grapes and black olives, meat, and a terracotta pitcher of wine, and from this he filled a goblet for her and topped up his own. Hers, when she raised it, was decorated in the image of her host with a tallish lady. She looked at him over the rim.

'Cheers,' he said, and drank.

'Cheers,' she replied, badly shocked, and drank too, a second shock. The wine tasted like syrup of figs or British sherry. Could it be *nectar*? Cheers indeed.

The velvety accented voice spoke again.

'You flew by Olympic?'

'Yes.' Really. Next he'd be telling her he was a director.

'You will stay for two weeks – fifteen days – yes? That is usual.'

His 'yes?' had the startling ring of the Mediterranean tourist tout, a hawker of hire cars and straw hats and boat trips round the bay. She felt equal and opposite and took courage.

'Do you spend much time in the islands?'

'In summer, yes, though it gets harder to find an empty

one. They come in their toy ships and swim around the shores with their rubber feet and their glass windows.

'Last week on the sacred island of Delos a girl from your land gave birth to a child. We felt the tremor on Olympus. Apollo visited the child with a disease and it died soon after. She had hair like a Maenad, the mother, and lived with others in a tent on the beach.'

'Hippies.'

'Please?'

'It's a general term for such people. They do no harm.'

Zeus snorted into his nectar and tore at some meat without offering her any. Mrs Paton took an olive in rebuke.

'Apollo is still alive then?'

'How could he be otherwise?'

She wanted to ask about Hera but it seemed indelicate. Zeus was wolfing the meat, chewing it with his mouth open, a habit she deplored. She must distract him before he took another mouthful. Politics, that was it. Greeks liked to talk politics.

'What do you think of the Revolutionary Government?'

'The Gods are above party politics.'

'But you must *think* about them?'

'Why? They never think of us. When our land was great it was not men who made it so. Not men unaided. They struggle now to find again the purpose of those days. They forget the purpose was never theirs.'

'Oh I do so agree,' said Mrs Paton. She had never voted, never expressed a political opinion in her life. She found it impossible to ally herself with the motives of her fellow men. People thought her stupid. But not Zeus. He listened most attentively as she outlined her philosophy, her conviction that society, not religion, was the opiate of the masses.

'People cling to each other because they are afraid to

contemplate infinity,' she said. And he nodded and refilled her goblet.

She decided to tell him about the intolerable materialism of life in the twentieth century. Of the hideous seductions of the consumer world so that, however long you held out against them, in the end your horizons too became cluttered with dishwashers and you warmed your heart with central heating and double glazing because there was nothing else to hope for, nothing.

Zeus told her about Jason and the Golden Fleece and she listened politely. 'But the Fleece was only the Means,' she said, 'double glazing is an End in itself,' and he had to agree.

She conjured for him the baying of the mob when you stepped outside it, the horror of bus parties where they made you sing, of staff dances and Woolworth's on Saturdays and Rothesay in July.

She described the country cottage she had found soon after her marriage, the thatch and the isolation and the long view over the moors and the arbour where she planned to build a shrine to Apollo. He looked piqued.

Then she told him of the house they had bought instead, of how she had imagined they were building her tomb as she watched it grow, brick by ugly brick, till it looked like every other in the street.

'You won't need a tomb now,' said Zeus, filling her goblet again.

Tears dripped into the wine as she relived her honeymoon in Pitlochry, her futile pregnancy, her failure to make close friends or successful sponge cakes, her short romance with a poodle till she killed it with overfeeding.

'It is better so,' said Zeus. 'Your time must not be taken up with trivia.'

She talked and he listened till the sun was the flaky dull

gold of an icon and the nectar a dying crescendo in her head.

She recalled her childhood. She had been an embarrassing child. They had had to carry her home from a matinee of *Snowhite* when she sobbed loudly at 'Some Day My Prince Will Come' and refused to be comforted by a choc ice. In her teens *The Flying Dutchman* had affected her the same way.

She had never fancied the local boys, nor indeed Mr Paton. She had held out stonily against the Dramatic Society and the church choir and the Townswomen's Guild.

'I always *knew* there was Something More,' she cried.

Zeus yawned, politely, behind his hand, and the gesture, so like Mr Paton's, plummeted her rudely back into the present.

'Oh dear,' she said, 'I have been going on. It must be the wine.' Indeed her face, when she touched it, was very hot, and her hair quite dishevelled and strawy.

'It *has* been nice meeting you,' she said, 'but I really must go.'

'No!' cried Zeus with an intensity that startled her. 'Not yet.' And a seabird, a grey seabird, swooped down on to a nearby rock and looked at them pointedly.

Zeus saw the bird too and his expression changed as he reached for something under the table. A parting gift? A statuette, maybe, or a nice vase?

It was a Japanese transistor set. How odd. He put it on the table between them and found some bouzouki music. Then he smiled at her. It was the first time he had smiled and it changed his face so dramatically it quite gave her the creeps.

'What is your name?'

'Phyllis.'

'Ph-y-ll-is.' The way he said it it might have been Desiree.

'I have waited for you a long time, Phyllis.'

'Really?'

'Poseidon combed the waves for you and Apollo swept the skies.'

'For me?'

'But it was foretold you would come along, stepping out of the waves on to the shore of this island we have kept for you.'

She looked about dazedly at the sand, the brown rocks, the small undistinguished hill that rose inland. Across the strait she could see another brown coastline with a white rectangle that must be the hotel.

'Why me?'

'Because you alone believe. On Olympus we felt your belief and grew strong because of it. Your sacrifices gave us the power to hope.'

She remembered the lamb cutlet, the handful of cornflakes tossed furtively into the Aga, the ear of barley picked in a field and laid out casually as for the birds.

'And now you are here as it was foretold. More beautiful by far than ever I had hoped, your hair as gold as never a mortal's that I saw before, your breasts two pink pillows, your . . .'

Inside, Mrs Paton began to freeze. Reflected in Zeus's eyes she saw a big pink middle-aged woman, gawky and diffident as a thirteen-year-old.

She tried to get up but her elbow collided with her goblet which emptied itself over the hand advancing towards her. Zeus licked it clean and began to fiddle with the transistor. Now Sinatra was competing with the bouzouki and some static, and his hands, both of them, were moving again across the table top. They were smooth, too smooth, and his breath smelt of garlic.

'Phyllis, lovely Phyllis, look at me.'

Mrs Paton blushed and fidgeted with the thunderbolt. It was small but heavy and her fingertips tingled when she touched it.

Zeus's hand, greasy with meat fat, came down purposefully on hers and she tingled all over.

'The time has come. All but two thousand years would pass, we knew, from the birth of him who turned man's minds from the Old Gods, till the coming of the New Mother . . .'

'*Mother?*'

Mrs Paton blushed right down under her swimsuit and tried to withdraw her hand. She failed. Her ears were ringing and softly through the din came the pulsating syllable . . . RE-LAX, RE-LAX, LIE BACK, LIE BACK . . . She shook her head to clear it. Zeus was still talking, holding her with his eye and his hand.

'Mother,' he was saying, 'mother of the first new God of the Second Coming, son of my Second Rule, seed of my loins, fruit of your womb . . .'

'*Stop it!*' screamed Mrs Paton and leaped to her feet, overturning the table. The thunderbolt slid on to the sand and the sky grew dark. As the first crash shook the heavens the wine spilt itself sizzling upon the thunderbolt and the rain began. It tore at her uncovered flesh and she crossed her arms over her chest. The wind came and blew the shattered pitcher, the grapes, the olive stones, until the beach looked like a Sunday picnic spot under the primeval terror of the storm.

Whimpering, Mrs Paton stood first on one leg, then the other, tucking them up like a frantic flamingo to save them from the stinging sand. They were all the same, even Gods. There was no place for her in the world or in the universe. She was alone, hopeless, ugly, doomed, mis-judged, violated. Apollo would never have treated her like this, nor Mr Paton.

'Greasey wop!' she screamed into the wind and abandoned herself to an ecstasy of self pity.

Zeus stood apart, powerless, his beard limp and dripping. Poseidon, helpless to intercede, raged around the world wrecking many ships. Hades beat his breast in fury and seismologists in many countries sent out warnings.

Only Sinatra remained unmoved, singing his little triumph from the wet sand, 'Love's been good to me.'

Zeus kicked the radio till he stopped.

'Cursed woman,' said Zeus to the seabird. 'I never had this trouble with the others.'

Athena shed her disguise and stood revealed in a white robe and gold sandals. Mrs Paton observed her secretly through her fingers as she snivelled and hiccuped.

'I can't think what went wrong,' Athena was saying. 'The wine, the music, the table for two, the good listening . . . That is the procedure. I have watched them. Perhaps you should have offered her presents? Money? Power?'

Zeus growled and the thunder echoed him. 'All-conquering Zeus does not bribe women. His favours are reward enough. And the prize of a place on Olympus.'

'What?' shouted Mrs Paton.

They turned to stare at her.

'Me? On Olympus?'

'Of course,' said Zeus. 'When I claim the child.'

Oh bliss. Oh joy. Oh vindication. Oh confusion to mortals. Home at last. Mrs Paton let out a sigh, a lifetime long.

Zeus raised his hand and the storm ceased.

And now Zeus and Mrs Paton stood alone on the beach.

'The child,' said Zeus, closing in, 'will go to Eton. I will claim him before the world on his eighteenth birthday.'

'And I will be truly immortal?'

'As I am,' said Zeus, yanking on her shoulder straps.

Mrs Paton fought him off. 'And I shall meet Apollo?'

'Yes yes,' said Zeus, discovering the miracle of the zip. But she had stopped fighting.

Afterwards, speeding back across the strait on the dolphin, Mrs Paton half expected to be chased by a gadfly. If she got through the next thirteen days it would be all right. Once back in Edinburgh Hera would find it hard to harry her. She must be on her guard against bolting horses and mad dogs. She doubted Hera would have the wit to adapt to speeding taxis, but if she did she had all the resources of the New World to pit against her.

Mr Paton was drinking ouzo on the terrace with Bill and Mavis, Lee and Sharon and the German couple, telling them about Edinburgh, the Athens of the North.

'Well well well,' he said, 'we were beginning to think you'd been struck by the lightning.'

'I was,' said Mrs Paton without blushing.

Golfers

Robin Jenkins

A famous professional recently stressed the importance to
golfers of shutting out the world and concentrating only
on the game. That this is sound advice is known even to
bunglers with handicaps of twenty-four. Whenever one of
these muffs a shot and the ball stots feebly in the wrong
direction he will nevertheless have been trying very hard
to think of absolutely nothing else but hitting it straight
and far: his crude technique has simply let him down.
Those figures in bright pullovers and spiked shoes, which
can be seen walking about a golf course as determined as
ants, are not human beings, they are golfers, concentrating on ball, stance and swing, to the exclusion of everything else. The best jokes in clubhouses celebrate this
fanatical but necessary single-mindedness.

Of the three hundred members of Auchenskeoch Golf
Club, on the west coast of Scotland, none appreciated the
necessity of total concentration more than a threesome
that played together every Saturday morning. It consisted
of William Lossit, manager of the local branch of the
Caledonia Bank, Jack Killeyan, principal teacher of
geography at Auchenskeoch High School, and Donald
McLairg, proprietor of the Clydeview Hotel. They had
met on the golf course and had taken care to keep their
acquaintance purely a golfing one. They did not visit one
another's houses and were not interested in one another's
affairs. Their wives knew one another to nod to in the
main street but were too well-trained ever to stop and

gossip. Instinctively they knew that in some mysterious way their husbands' golf would suffer if they got to know one another well. Thus, after five years of playing together, the three men remained staunchly strangers.

Unless the rain was tempestuous or snow blanketed the course, they would meet on the first tee at half-past nine. After exchanging nods and good-mornings, they would toss to see who should have the honour of driving off first, and immediately begin. During the game they might mention, perfunctorily, some tournament of world-famous professionals taking place elsewhere, and the other two might grunt in commendation if the third brought off some spectacularly good shot; but for the most part they kept quiet and concentrated on the golf.

William Lossit had been a bank manager for ten years. Headquarters in Edinburgh, and some of his customers, now and then were not satisfied with his management, but in a time of fallen standards anyone not downright incompetent was secure. So he was content in his red-tiled bungalow with its fine view of Arran. He liked to work in the garden, taking care not to get calluses on his hands that might interfere with the proper gripping of his golf clubs. His grown-up son, happily married, was flourishing in Inverness as a chartered accountant. He had only one worry, if it could be called that. It concerned his wife, Agnes. For months on end she would be the perfect wife, obedient, dutiful, thrifty and self-effacing; then suddenly she would go and do something odd. It was never anything sensational, indeed it was always trifling. For instance, he would plant some gladioli in some spot he had carefully chosen. In a day or two he would discover she had dug them up and replanted them in some other place quite unsuitable. Then again, he was fond of a certain brand of sauce. Once when the bottle was empty she replaced it with a different brand altogether, one she must have known he would not like. Over the years there had been many such oddities of behaviour on her part. Sometimes he wondered if their purpose could be to spite him, perhaps in revenge for his devoting more time to golf than to her.

As a teacher, Jack Killeyan was no more and no less successful than the majority of his colleagues. Given a bright class, he got good results; given a dull one, his results were poor.

He had been glad when he had got the post at Auchenskeoch: there was an increase in salary; the troublemakers of Auchenskeoch were less vicious and enterprising than those of Glasgow, whence he had come and where he had been born; the seaside air was healthier for his two daughters, and the golf course at Auchenskeoch was a splendid one, running alongside the sea.

After eight years at Auchenskeoch, his contentment was ruined when he noticed, or rather when his wife Bessie noticed, that contemporaries of his, in no observable way superior, were being promoted to headmasterships. He thereupon began to apply for every appropriate post he saw advertised, from Thurso in the north to Kelso in the south. Bessie helped him to fill in the forms. Unfortunately, she could not be with him at his interviews, to tell him what to say and, still more important, what not to say. Unknown to him, she wrote to their daughters, one by this time a nurse in Glasgow and the other a student in Edinburgh, that Dad was getting a bit depressed about being rejected so often, but they weren't to mention it, and anyway he had his golf to console and sustain him.

Donald McLairg had inherited Clydeview Hotel from his

father. It was large, and occupied an enviable position near the harbour, though the roses in its front gardens seemed to smell of seaweed. Like Auchenskeoch itself, it was a little run down, suffering, like all Clydeside hotels, from the preference of Glaswegians for the sunshine of Majorca to the rain and midges of the Scottish Riviera.

In his young days Donald had loved to go off to watch the Open Championship wherever it was being played. He had stayed in the same five-star hotels as some of the famous competitors, and spent a lot of money. He had also been fond of pinching the bottoms of the Clydeview maids. Since then he had unaccountably married Martha, as skinny as she was devout. There was no mention of golf in the Bible, so she couldn't make up her mind whether or not the Lord approved of it. Consequently, Donald was allowed to continue, though he was obliged to wear less flamboyant pullovers and hats. After a while, his bottom-pinching was resumed, furtively.

On a certain Saturday in early September, with the sun shining mellowly and the course in delectable condition, the threesome met on the first tee, making practice swings with customary zest, and handling their golf balls with the same old delight and anticipation. Or so it appeared. The truth was, none of the three that morning was going to find it easy to shut out the world and concentrate on the game.

On the previous afternoon, Mrs Lossit had come into her husband's office at the bank, carrying her shopping-bag. There was no stated rule, but he did not approve of her bothering him at work. Besides, he had a customer coming in to discuss Unit Trusts.

While he was hinting as fondly as he could about the inconvenience of her intrusion, she made things worse by taking out of her bag, and setting down on his desk, such absurd objects as a bobbin of purple thread, a card of white elastic, a packet of needles, and a tin of ointment. For a few moments he gave his attention to this assortment. He jaloused she intended to replace the elastic in her knickers, say, and he tried to remember if she had a pair purplish in colour. The ointment baffled him. He was about to ask her to take them off his desk when she remarked, casually, that she hadn't paid for them, she had just shoplifted them out of Woolworth's. She didn't know whether anyone had seen her.

Immediately he saw his career in jeopardy. At any moment there would be a knock on the door and in would come Jim Chapman, manager of Woolworth's, followed by Sergeant Moffat and a constable. Agnes would be charged. The case would go before Bob Aitchison, the Sheriff, a member of the Golf Club. If a plea of temporary insanity was put forward she might get off with a fine or even an admonition. But there would be a full account in the *Auchenskeoch Observer*. The whole town, nay the whole county, would wonder if a man whose wife had been found guilty of shoplifting was fit to manage a bank. Everybody would think he had been mean with the housekeeping money.

With an effort he turned his concern from himself to poor Agnes, still surveying with silly pride her pathetic booty. He hated her then, but he also loved her more poignantly than he had done for years. She was so familiar and yet so strange. He saw pain in her eyes where, that very morning, at breakfast, he had seen only wilful obtuseness. He noticed now how thin and shaky her hands were in their black gloves. He had looked after his golf clubs more carefully than he had her. Whatever her present condition, he was partly to blame for it.

* * *

That same Friday, Jack Killeyan was in Aberdeen for an interview. Always, before those interviews, and alas, during them, he was so worked up that he could scarcely force words past his lips, and they were never his best words. Once again he did not do himself justice; but this time his failure left him sickened and demoralized. Among the other candidates was a man he'd worked beside in Glasgow years ago, a notorious work-dodger with a glib tongue. Saunders had been the one appointed. The Aberdeen councillors were not to blame. They had been hoodwinked. The system was at fault, allowing the best man to be passed over and the worst chosen.

Returning in his car to Auchenskeoch, he wept. Tears dribbled down his cheeks. Not even Bessie would ever know about them. He would as always pretend he wasn't a bit hurt or downhearted. His sense of humour, he would say, enabled him, thank God, to laugh at the absurdity of a scrimshanker like Harry Saunders being made a headmaster.

That night Bessie was unable to comfort him. Like the unjealous wife she was, she hoped golf would do it, as it had done often in the past.

About three months before a new barmaid had been engaged for the Clydeview cocktail bar. Since his wife was the hirer, Donald was astonished to find that the new employee was the kind of woman he yearned for. Nancy Cameron was big, with magnificent bosom and ample buttocks. But it was the quality of her flesh that thrilled him, it was so soft, luscious and perfumed. His own melted at the sight of it, more so at the feel of it, for in the closed space behind the bar his haunch could hardly avoid nudging hers. He found himself pouring drams of unprecedented generosity. Suddenly the lounge with its few poinsettias bloomed like Eden. He was in love. Her blonde hair was dyed, but it didn't matter.

She was divorced and living in a rented room-and-kitchen in the working-class end of the town. One wet night he offered to run her home in his car. Her street was deserted. Hand on his knee, she asked him up. He mumbled his car would be seen. She suggested he could drive it to the front nearby, where it would never be noticed among the cars of holiday makers.

Here was a situation overwhelming for a furtive bottom-pincher. Mumbling what he thought was a rejection of her offer, but which she took to be an acceptance, he drove off, intending to head straight for the safe dullness of home, but finding himself, to his alarm, on the sea-front.

He crouched in his car for ten minutes, trying to fight off the temptation. He saw how abominably foolish it would be for him to put in peril his respectability as a citizen and church-goer and husband, not to mention his career as a golfer. He recalled his triumphs on the golf course, especially his winning of the Auchenskeoch Trophy. That had been the proudest time in his life. He smiled bravely and told himself that the man who had then received the silver cup from Provost Paible, with dozens applauding, would hardly be so stupid as to ruin himself for the sake of half an hour in the company of a woman who, however luscious, was nevertheless just a barmaid, and divorced at that. All the time he knew, as men in such situations nearly always do, that he would in the end sneak through the rain to No. 53 Westfield Street.

She was expecting him in the little kitchen. She wore a short pink negligee and furry slippers. A whisky bottle and glasses were on the table. There was a blazing coal fire. There was also a set-in bed.

Speaking in a soothing yet cheerful voice, she encouraged him to talk at length about his ambitions and achievements as a golfer. She had heard, she said, he had been a great player in his day, and still was a pretty good one, considering his age. Not that he was too old for golf, or for anything else she could think of.

He stayed three hours, and made love to her in the set-in bed. So kind her voice, and so hospitable her body, his fears and scruples were, for the short time it took, easily routed by joy.

Martha was asleep when he crept into their bedroom. She woke up and, to his amazement, swallowed his lie that he had been with golfing friends. Yawning, she went back to sleep. He felt greatly relieved, but also, so irrepressible is self, a little displeased and disappointed that she should so readily consider him incapable of any tremendous defiance of respectability. Before falling asleep, he lay and shuddered, knowing that he might have put himself into a blackmailer's power; but amidst the shudders were little shivers of remembered joy.

During the following week he kept out of Nancy's way. She made it easy by not pursuing him. When they did meet she merely winked. If she thought she had a claim on him, she was going to take her time about asserting it. Then, suddenly, she was gone, sacked by Martha. 'I'm not saying she was brazen, but she's the kind could be.' He waited, in terror, for Nancy to come and demand that he speak up for her, otherwise she'd tell; but she was content with a smile, on her way out. He watched her go, with relief and regret chasing each other round his mind.

Discreetly speiring, he heard she'd left the town and gone to Greenock.

Then, on the same Friday that Mrs Lossit took to shop-lifting and Jack Killeyan saw the triumph of the unworthy, Donald was called to the telephone. To his horror, the voice was Nancy's, as kind and cheerful as ever. She wanted to see him. She had something interesting to tell him. He'd find her on a seat near the paddling pool.

He went, with twenty pounds in his pocket to buy her off. He whimpered to himself what a reckless, trusting fool he had been.

On the green bench she looked beautiful in a bright red costume and red shoes. She seemed relaxed, and gave him a wave that couldn't have been more friendly or even loving.

'Hello, Daddy,' she whispered, cheerily.

No greeting could have flummoxed him more. He and Martha had no children, and never would have. He was fond of children, though. Nancy must have seen him joking with them at the hotel.

She laid her hand on her stomach. 'I'm pregnant, love.'

People were passing. Beyond them shone the sea. If she was telling the truth he would have to drown himself. The view from the seventh tee flashed into his mind. There were cliffs and seabirds. A badly hooked drive could land you in the sea.

He recovered his wits. 'You can't be.'

'I may be divorced, love, but I've still got my ovaries.'

'Are you sure? Have you seen a doctor?'

'Missed twice, love. No doctor could tell better than that.'

'All right. But what's it got to do with me?'

She laughed, but not sarcastically. 'Quite a lot. It's yours.'

'So you say. It could be some other man's.'

'When it's born you'll see it's got sandy hair and big ears.'

Lots of men had sandy hair and big ears, he could have told her, but didn't, she would have found it funny. He had never seen a woman so carefree.

'You don't look at all worried.'

'Why should I be worried, love? A wee sister, or a wee brother, for Melinda. That's how I look at it.'

'Who's Melinda?'

'My girl. She's eight. That's her, in the blue coat.'

The little girl was neat and bonny. He would have been proud to be her father.

'I didn't know you had a daughter.'

'Donald, you and me are practically strangers, more's the pity, even if we've been intimate, as they say in the divorce courts.'

But from the way she laughed she bore no more spite against those courts than she did against him.

'What do you want me to do?'

'Nothing, love. You've got your wife to think of. She needs you. I just thought you should know. Some day, maybe, if you'd like, I could bring him or her and let you have a look.'

It was too astonishing a prospect for him to know whether he would like it or not.

'Don't worry, love. I'll not embarrass you. I like you too much. You're my kind of fellow. You and me could have made a great pair. Well, here's Melinda. Melinda, this is my friend, Mr McLairg.'

He exchanged smiles with the little girl. He wondered if her half-brother or half-sister would look like her.

Nancy rose. She seemed just a little agitated. 'Got to go, love. Best of luck.'

He watched them ambling along the sea-front, hand-in-hand, the big fine-looking woman in the red costume, and the dainty little girl in the blue coat. They turned twice to wave. He was almost in tears. He suspected he was losing something more valuable than gold or golf.

No golfer, or golfer's wife, will marvel that men with such burdens on their minds should turn up that Saturday morning to hit a small white ball from one distant hole to another. Golf is not so much a game as an addiction.

It never occurred to William Lossit not to play that morning. He had left Agnes alone so often that it had become a habit. In any case, he felt that with his clubs in his hands he would be better able to steady his mind, so that afterwards he would know what to do about Agnes. It could well be that if he was a little more overt in his displays of affection, she would cease her pathetic attempts to persecute him. Or it could be that firmness was required, or at least a determination to stop her from hiding herself from him in the depths of her mind. She ought not to have given up golf. For a woman of her build she had played not badly.

Well, he thought, as he got out of his car, rejoicing to see the course shining in the sun, he was only her husband after all, not the keeper of her soul.

Jack Killeyan was tenderly kissed by his wife at the door. 'Don't take it too sorely to heart,' she whispered. Just like a woman, he reflected, as he drove to the course. He had been given proof of a rottenness in society, and she wanted him not to let it bother him. Bessie was a good woman and a loyal wife, she cleaned his shoes and knitted his pullovers, but she had no understanding of principle. When he had said he was minded to write to the *Glasgow Herald,* exposing the injustices inherent in the present system of promoting teachers, she had been horrified. All the authorities in Scotland would read it, she'd whispered. His name would be marked. There would be no use his applying ever again, anywhere. No one would say he'd done it out of principle; everybody would say it was sour grapes. Best write nothing. Best give the impression you thought the system was fair enough. Best keep applying and hoping. That had been her advice, and he found it all the more insulting because of course he intended to follow it.

Several other players were at the first tee waiting their turn. They looked on with interest as our threesome prepared to drive off. McLairg, Lossit and Killeyan were known to have been very low handicap men in their heyday, McLairg's name in fact was up on the champions' board in the clubhouse, and they all still played off four or five. They were scrutinized therefore, not as men and citizens, but as golfers whose swings were still worth analysing.

Lossit and Killeyan watched too as their partner drove off. For the first time in years they saw him as a man. To Lossit he was the husband of a sensible, business-like woman. To Killeyan he was the owner of a substantial hotel, independent therefore, and removed from the rat-race of promotion.

As McLairg's ball flew straight down the fairway for a good two hundred and thirty yards, his partners, nodding appreciation, at the same time thought how unfair it was that this red-cheeked, unimaginative native of Auchenskeoch hadn't a care between his big ears. It gave him a three-stroke advantage, at least.

Killeyan, watching Lossit drive, thought the bank manager too was lucky, in that he belonged to a profession where promotion depended on merit, not on chance or glibness. He attributed therefore to a jerky swing the surprising rightward deviation of Lossit's ball, which landed in the midst of whins, where it could well be lost.

Watching Killeyan's ball fly far and true, Lossit thought gloomily how he too could have hit a good shot if, at the moment of striking, he had had a picture of his wife smiling adoringly, like Killeyan's, instead of hurrying into Auchenskeoch as soon as his back was turned, for some more shoplifting, or worse.

As he strode over the turf, McLairg was hardly aware of
his two companions, even as golfers. He had satisfied
himself that there was no danger of Martha's ever finding
out about his child. Therefore he felt free to savour the
joy and glory of becoming a father. Under his shoes were
tiny violet flowers he had seen dozens of times before but
had never really noticed until now. He wished he knew
their name. Then, when he was poking among the whins
in search of Lossit's ball, and saw there were still a few
yellow flowers on the bushes, he recalled the saying that
kissing would be out of favour when the whins were out of
flowers. He felt so delighted that he did not search as
diligently as he ought, and neither, he observed, did
Killeyan, with the result that Lossit, visibly peeved at so
poor a beginning, had to declare his ball lost and go all the
way back to the tee and drive another.

They always played for a stake. Each man put a pound
into the kitty and the winner took all. It was a small
amount for prosperous men, and never before had
brought temper or grudge into the game. McLairg therefore was surprised when, on the sixth green, Killeyan
putted to within fourteen inches of the hole, and was
about to pick up his ball assuming the next putt had been
conceded, when Lossit snarled at him to putt it out. Lossit
of course was within his golfing rights, it was conceivable
Killeyan could miss the putt, especially as he wasn't
putting well so far, but even so these small concessions
were customary. McLairg wondered if the bank manager
was ill, or more likely if his wife was; but it wasn't his
business, particularly on the golf course, and so he gave it
no more thought.

Killeyan hated to be playing badly, especially when
someone else was playing very well; and when that
someone was a big, hen-pecked, thick-headed fellow
who'd been lucky enough to fall heir to a thriving hotel, it

was all the more disagreeable. Usually too, the hotel owner was solemn when playing, fatuously so sometimes, whereas this morning he kept grinning and chuckling. Once, when waiting for Killeyan to play – the ball was lying unfairly in a divot mark – McLairg went down on his hunkers nearby to pluck and hold to his nose a tiny flower. Killeyan knew golfers who would have regarded that squatting and sniffing as provocation, or at least distraction.

As for Lossit, Killeyan was becoming slowly aware that here was a man he could easily dislike. He remembered something Bessie had said about Mrs Lossit. 'She's a poor soul. I wouldn't be surprised if she had a bad pain somewhere. He never seems to notice.' Well, was a man who never noticed his wife was ill, might have cancer, was such a man fit to play golf, morally speaking?

That almost metaphysical question occurred to Killeyan as he stood on the seventh tee. Of all the tees on the course this was the one where he ought to have concentrated, eyes, heart and soul, on the ball. On the left were cliffs, in front was a deep gully. Elderly or nervous members by-passed that tee. But never once had Killeyan, in his previous dozens of games, sent the ball to disaster. This morning, though, his mind on moral matters, he swung too fast and hit the ball, not over the cliffs or into the gully, but into thick heather.

A bad shot always brings a feeling of shame. He slunk off, avoiding the gazes of his companions.

If he had told them why he had duffed that drive, that he had suddenly been seized by a sense of his own unworthiness, as golfer and man, they would not have sympathized, on the contrary they would have been offended by his bringing up on the golf course too important and personal a matter. If he had said a midge had got into his eye they would have nodded, in understanding and sympathy.

So humbled did he feel, and yet so well-disposed towards

his fellow-men, whether they played golf or not, that when he came up to Lossit on the fairway he couldn't resist saying, 'Well, William, isn't it a glorious morning?'

'Aye,' grunted Lossit. He was concentrating.

As Killeyan waited he heard skylarks and seagulls, and saw the sun shining on the Arran peaks.

Lossit's ball came to rest on the green no more than ten feet from the pin. McLairg's was already there, even closer. Killeyan's own was in a bunker, but what did it matter?

'Donald's in great fettle today,' he said, as he and Lossit walked towards the green.

'Aye.'

Lossit had noticed Killeyan was preoccupied. Perhaps he had been having trouble with some truculent pupils. It was said in the town he tried to reason with louts, and failed sadly.

But Lossit did not want to think about Killeyan. Happy memories of Agnes had begun to occur to him. He could not say why. He had done nothing to evoke them. He remembered her in their son's garden in Inverness, playing with her three-year-old granddaughter. She had looked twenty years younger.

When it was his turn to putt and he had to clear everything out of his mind except line and distance, he found he did not want to stop remembering Agnes chasing wee Sheila among the roses. As a consequence his mind was divided. It was no surprise therefore when he did not strike the ball well and it stopped still two and a half feet from the hole. What was a surprise, though, was that he did not feel aggrieved or disappointed. It just seemed, for a visionary moment, unimportant, compared with that happy memory of Agnes.

As they were walking to the next tee, he wanted to go on remembering Agnes at Inverness. He was not pleased therefore when Killeyan, who seemed to be seeking reassurance of some sort, came alongside him, determined to speak.

'Would you say Walter Hagen was right? Remember what he said? "You should always take time of. to smell the roses." When playing golf, he meant.'

'I know what he meant,' replied Lossit, crossly, though as before he did not feel cross. How could he, when he had been reminded of his own roses at home, so much admired by neighbours? Agnes used to make pot-pourri with the fallen petals.

'It hardly applies here,' he said, more amiably. 'There aren't any roses on the course.'

'Well, maybe not in September.'

'Not at any time, so far as I know.'

'In July there are. Wild roses.'

'Wild roses? On the course?'

Killeyan laughed. 'One bush. In the hollow to the right at the sixteenth tee. It's not much of a bush, and its leaves are rusted with the salt breezes, but it does have flowers. I've seen them.'

Yet he had never troubled to point them out. 'Even so,' said Lossit. 'Wild roses have no scent.'

Killeyan laughed again. 'Roses were just a symbol,' he said. 'Here, what would he have said?' He raised his head and gazed round. 'He could have said the sea, or the Arran hills, or the lighthouse yonder.'

They were on the tee now, standing judiciously apart from McLairg, who had his ball teed up ready to drive.

'Of course,' whispered Killeyan, 'he meant between shots.'

He winked, and Lossit found himself winking back. They were amused by the absurdity of any golfer thinking of roses or hills or lighthouses when about to play a shot.

They felt closer to each other than ever before, closer indeed than either of them wished.

Lossit thought that Killeyan, in spite of his typically schoolmasterish assumption of knowing everything, was well enough intentioned. He would never make a headmaster, though. He lacked authority. He hadn't enough confidence in himself. His wife told him what to do.

Killeyan thought that perhaps the reason why the bank manager found it hard to make friends wasn't because he had too high an opinion of himself, which was the town's view of him, but because, like McLairg, he lacked imagination. It was said Mrs Lossit was once a cheerful woman, as well as an enthusiastic golfer. She had wilted like a plant deprived of sunshine. A man without imagination was bound to have the same effect on his wife.

Killeyan felt encouraged. Even if all his subsequent applications and interviews were failures he would have the consolation of knowing that his wife was a happy, benevolent woman. While it would be arrogant for him to claim that it was his imaginativeness which had kept Bessie so fresh and bonny, he had a right to think it had played a part.

No man was given everything. There was McLairg, beaming after another splendid drive: he owned a big hotel, he was still a fine golfer, but his wife was plain and skinny, and he had no children.

As for Lossit, he might well be promoted to a larger bank in a larger town, and his son Ian was doing very well as a chartered accountant, but his wife was ailing and depressed, and he had no imagination.

From then on their play was often held up by slow-coaches in front. There were opportunities for conversations which Lossit was afraid Killeyan would seize. He was afraid only as a golfer anxious not to ruin his score; as a man he too wanted to talk. Indeed, it was he who spoke, as they stood waiting on the twelfth fairway.

Once again, McLairg kept aloof from them. They understood and approved. Heading for an excellent score, he did not want to be distracted by their chatter.

'I believe Mrs Killeyan helps out in the Ox-fam shop these days,' said Lossit, pleasantly.

'Yes. Every Thursday afternoon.'

'Do you approve?'

He was puzzled by the astonishment on Killeyan's face.

'Why not?' said Killeyan, laughing. 'Anyway, I wasn't asked.'

Lossit was surprised by the man's levity and shallowness. 'One has to be very careful,' he said, 'how one helps people. Otherwise there is a danger one might take away from them their independence and initiative, with the result that for the rest of their lives they'll go on expecting to be helped.'

'You could be right, but I don't see how it can apply to starving children. Well, that's the green clear now.'

It was true the green was clear and the game could be resumed, but Lossit felt sure Killeyan had broken off the subject because he was shocked by Lossit's intelligent realism. Famine was ghastly, but it could be nature's way of drastically reducing populations that needed to be drastically reduced.

But it would not do to think of famine when hitting a golf ball. Therefore, with a smile, Lossit suspended thought on the subject, and concentrated on making sure he hit the ball neither to the right where the sea shore was out of bounds nor to the left where there was a bank with grass a foot tall. He swung smoothly. The ball flew straight. It came to rest on the green. It was a fine shot.

Killeyan's was not so good. His ball fell well short of the green. He had hit it half-heartedly. He must have been thinking of those starving children. Lossit smiled, and went on smiling when Killeyan, in too big a hurry, got the wheels of their caddy-cars entangled.

'Sorry,' muttered Killeyan, his eyes on the ground. 'By the way, Bessie was saying she wondered if Mrs Lossit would like to help. They need volunteers. She says being a banker's wife Mrs Lossit will be good at handling money.'

No doubt Mrs Killeyan had meant no sarcasm when making the remark, nor had Killeyan when repeating it. They had no way of knowing that Agnes was hopeless with money, so much so that it was he who calculated each week's budget. If she bought a new dress or coat he wrote out the cheque. It occurred to him, as he glanced down at his pale green cashmere pullover, bought last week for £12.50, that it had been a long time since Agnes had bought herself anything new to wear. He had been pleased with her thrift, but he realized now he should have insisted she buy herself some new clothes. As his wife she ought not to have let herself become dowdy. Perhaps it had been part of her campaign to make him pay attention to her. Poor Agnes.

For the next five holes they did not speak. Lossit was able to concentrate on his golf, but Killeyan evidently couldn't, judging from the number of bad shots he played. On the sixteenth tee Lossit had to look for the rosebush himself. Killeyan did not offer to point it out.

McLairg, sensible man, had taken no interest in their conversations. He was in sparkling form, hitting the ball better than they had seen him do in years. He would have been stupid to let anything divide his attention. His sniffs at the flower had really been sniffs at the course; it had been his way of stimulating his golfing instincts.

It seemed to Lossit that another advantage of having a wife to whom you could confidently leave all your business worries was that, on the golf course, you could put her completely out of your mind. Not that he would have exchanged Agnes for Martha McLairg. Agnes had once been a cheerful woman, Martha never. Agnes could be made cheerful again.

Killeyan had known at the back of his mind that McLairg was scoring well. He was marking McLairg's card and had been putting down many fours and more threes than fives; but he had only a vague idea that McLairg was heading for a really remarkable score.

As they were waiting on the eighteenth tee, he totted it up. He could not believe the total he arrived at, and tried again, with the same astounding result. If McLairg managed a four at the eighteenth, which was possible, he would have an overall score of 68. The par for the course was 72. The record, held by a Glasgow professional, was 66, though that of course was from the medal tees.

Killeyan was so impressed he showed the card to Lossit.

'Donald needs a four for a 68,' he whispered.

'I knew he must have a very good score,' whispered Lossit.

McLairg, as usual, was first to drive. He was practising his swing.

'Donald,' called Killeyan, 'do you know you need a four here for a sixty-eight?'

It was, as he and Lossit knew, a rhetorical question. Only golfers playing badly are vague about their scores. They expected McLairg to nod, with a golfer's curt modesty, and then to turn again and stare, with a golfer's impatience, at the poldders in front who were holding him up. They were astonished therefore when he smiled, shyly it seemed, and spoke.

'How's Ian getting on these days, Mr Lossit?' he asked. 'He's in Inverness, isn't he?'

Lossit was pleased as well as astonished. 'Yes. He's doing very well, thank you.'

'He would. Smart lad. Married, isn't he?'

'Yes.'

'Any family?'

'One wee girl.'

'He got married, didn't he, before he finished his training?'

'They all do these days, Donald.'

'A wee girl, eh? That's good. Mr Killeyan there knows all about wee girls. He's got two.'

'What's this Mr Killeyan nonsense?' said Killeyan. 'Name's Jack. Yes, I've got two. But they're not wee girls any longer, sorry to say. One's twenty and the other's twenty-three nearly.'

'I remember the younger one,' said McLairg. 'Plump little girl, with straight black hair?'

'That's Jeanie. She's not so plump now she's a nurse. She's to work too hard.'

'Donald,' murmured Lossit, 'they've moved on. You can hit off now.'

He had to mention it, because they too were being closely pursued by another threesome. He looked at Killeyan with apology for having interrupted the conversation, and Killeyan nodded, with a smile, expressing agreement that the game was the first consideration.

'Take it easy,' they advised McLairg, afraid lest the talk about their children should have upset him, who was childless. Besides, if he scored a 68 they too would share a little in the glory.

He drove. It was his best drive of the morning. Right down the middle of the fairway it flew. When it landed it ran on and on. From where it stopped was only an eight or nine iron shot to the green. His 68 looked almost a certainty now.

Their own drives were more than satisfactory. No matter how bad one's score, it was always gratifying to do well at the eighteenth, for members sitting in the clubhouse were sure to be watching critically.

They walked together up the fairway.

Killeyan thought that, if McLairg was lucky to have no promotion disappointments, he was also without malice or conceit. In fact, he was that combination that school-teachers often thanked God for in their pupils: slowness of mind compensated for by a happy and well-disposed nature.

Lossit thought that while McLairg was fortunate to have a sensible and business-like wife he deserved credit for the fact that she had remained sensible and business-like. Married to a less patient and more ambitious man, she might well have developed into a religious bigot.

Both of them felt sorry for McLairg. He had no children and yet he would have made a good father.

Their charitable moods were confirmed when they both had fine second shots and landed their balls safely on the green. They could not help exchanging congratulatory grins.

They tood still as stones as McLairg shaped up to play his shot. They prayed he would not strike the ball into the burn that ran alongside the fairway. To spoil his score now would be lamentable.

Suddenly, to their amazement, he stepped back and held up his club, a nine-iron, above his head, as if it was a spear, about to be hurled at the distant clubhouse, or the world beyond. Members watching must have thought he'd been attacked by a bee or even an adder.

Killeyan and Lossit knew there was no bee or snake. They could not understand what had come over him. Up till now he had behaved with exemplary golfing saneness. Why was he now acting more like a Zulu warrior than a golfer?

Except that the smile on his face was the very opposite of hostile or murderous. He looked inspiredly happy, as if, thought Killeyan, he had just discovered how to feed all the starving children without destroying their independence. It could hardly be a score of 68 that was causing such transcendental joy. Golf after all was only a game and had its limits.

When McLairg, moments later, strode up to the ball he was a golfer again. His swing was crisp. The ball glittered in the sunshine, and came to rest close to the flag on the green. Only one putt would be needed. He would have gone round in 67.

In awe Killeyan and Lossit wondered what marvellous thing could have been in their companion's mind to inspire him to hit so confident a shot.

When they arrived on the green they saw the critical faces at the clubhouse windows. Each of them therefore, as he studied his line and then as he crouched over his putter, was very remote as a man but intimately close as a golfer. Killeyan's putt stopped three inches from the hole, Lossit's six, and McLairg's went straight in. It was as masterly a conclusion to a game of golf as any threesome could have prayed for. Those watching from the clubhouse looked satisfied.

In spite of the sweetness of that last hole, Killeyan had taken 88 strokes and Lossit 82. Usually it was bitter not to be under 80, but somehow not today. Both of them felt dimly but strongly that they had achieved something more important than golfing success, though of course they could not say so openly, less the sincerity of their congratulations to McLairg be suspect.

They always went straight home. They were not drinking men, and even beer in the middle of the day seemed to them not quite proper. McLairg, though, often went into the bar for a whisky and a chat.

Today, as they shook hands and thanked one another for the game, McLairg, his big red face beaming, invited them in for a drink.

'To celebrate,' he said.

Somehow they got the impression he wasn't referring to his magnificent score.

Killeyan muttered he would like to but he'd promised his wife he'd be home by one-thirty; it was after that now; he really shouldn't keep her waiting any longer.

Lossit nodded, as if that was his reason too for having to hurry home.

Like the amiable chap he was, and like a magnanimous golfer who had just broken 70, McLairg accepted their excuses without fuss.

'Next Saturday then, gentlemen?' he asked.

Ever so briefly, they hesitated. Past his big ears they gazed at the sunlit course. They thought how stale life would seem without golf to look forward to. To give it up would be like giving up hope.

'Next Saturday, Donald,' they said, firmly and confidently.

You Don't Come the Pickle
with the Onion

Peter Chaloner

If you want to understand what happened you've got to understand this. The Professor couldn't get it. But it's that simple a wee child could get it. *I am a thief.* Simple as that. If I see something I want, and there's nobody about, I'll take it. It's not right, I know that. But you do a lot of things that are not right.

I'm proud to be a thief. Just the same as I'm proud to be Scottish. If there's a war starts tomorrow I'll be down there asking for my rifle. Folk might say I'm daft but I don't bother. It's my belief. It's my way – like having a job. I could get on the Social Security tomorrow if I wanted. But I prefer getting up early and going down to the wood-yard. The money's rubbish, but I don't care. It's me. I know what I am.

Now the Professor, he never knew what I was. To him I was just somebody simple, somebody needing brought on. He thought I was a clear case of pig ignorance, to tell you the Christ's truth. But I proved to him that my head doesn't zip up the back. You might say it was hard on him. But you don't come the pickle with the onion.

The first time I spoke to him I was careful to be very polite. I chapped his door with my bottle of wine very quietly. When he came I talked to him like he was the police.

'Not being cheeky or anything,' I says, 'but I heard the music from down below and I just thought I'd come up and offer you a drink. Not being cheeky or anything. But

I'm awful fond of music, so I am.' Polite you'll notice. But casual with it. I didn't let on that it was a surprise to hear somebody up our way playing a tune. I just acted as if there's real music up our close every night of the week. But the fact is there hasn't been such a thing for years.

It's all old property, our street. All to come down. Most people have moved out, and our close is like the rest – only three houses have got folk in them. Used to be there were twelve. It's not the sort of place you expect to hear music. Not real music. Anyway, this night my mother's asleep, and I'm sitting in the house on my own with a couple of cans and a bottle of wine, as usual. And all of a sudden – music. Real bagpipe music. It'd near enough deafen you – I knew right away it wasn't a record or the telly. It seemed to be coming from up the stair. I didn't recognize the tune, but I starts humming along all the same. It's a thing I love to hear, the pipes. Only one thing I like better and that's an accordion. Then I think to myself, Davie, who is that, playing that? The only people I knew to be up the stair were the Macs, an old couple, real hard up. The last thing they'd do would be go out and buy a pair of bagpipes. And nobody ever came to see them. I knew it couldn't be them. So there was only one thing for it. Somebody must have moved into one of the empty flats next door to them. There were two doors up there, still not boarded up. The people were not long away.

It was hard to believe that anybody would move in. I mean, that anybody could be that stupid. There's a man from the Corporation round every couple of weeks to see if the whole building needs demolished. Unsafe. But somebody must have done it. The music was there and that loud the whole street must be hearing it. So I says to myself, Davie, what are you going to do? Sit down here humming to yourself, like an old alky? Or get up there beside whoever it is playing the music? So up I go.

The Professor was about as old as my dad, but skinny. I noticed that when he opened the door. Skinny all over, and red-faced, even although this was October. You would never have taken him for anything special. Of course at this point I didn't know he was a Professor. To me he was just an old guy in a wool shirt and brown woolly trousers and old cord slippers with holes at the toes. Perfectly ordinary. Only one thing unusual about him was he looked as if he was thinking too hard. He seemed to look beyond you more than at you, as if he could see something behind your back that was making him think twice. Apart from that, there wasn't a brainy-looking thing about him.

'Come in,' he says, after I says my piece. No smile. No palaver. So I was in.

I know he'd probably only moved in that day, but you should have seen the state his house was in. Ours is just the same size – room and kitchen and inside toilet – but in our place we've got comfort built up over the years. Him! In the kitchen, he'd got broken-down old furniture stacked up to the ceiling. That's no exaggeration. Up to the ceiling. Broken-legged tables, burst wardrobes, arm-chairs with springs hanging out – it was like the pictures you see of the barricades in the Easter Rising. Just a path about five feet wide to let him in to the gas cooker. The last folk would have left it all behind fair enough, but he could have made a wee bit effort. Then in the room – we went through because there was a gas fire on in there – next to nothing. Just a sleeping bag on a mattress on the bare floorboards. An old sheet pinned up at the window. And a plank of wood across two low stacks of bricks for a bench. His bagpipes were on the bed, beside a battered old suitcase like the sanitary man carries around. As we came in he picked them up, and we both sat on the bench, and I got the top off my wine. I offered it to him first but he was doing something to his chanter so I took the first drink myself. Still he hadn't said a word apart from 'Come in'.

'I'm Davie,' I said. I don't believe in saying nothing. Not when you've just met a bloke. 'My mother and father have lived in that house down the stair for forty years. Brought seven of us up there. I wasn't meaning to be cheeky or that, but I heard the music and I says to myself if you get in you get in, and if you don't why worry? Eh? Know what I mean?'

But he wasn't bothering listening to me.

He stands up with the pipes on his shoulder and the chanter in his hand, then he looks at me – or I should say, at the space behind me.

'You say you're a lover of music,' he says.

I was a bit taken aback at his voice. Just like mine. Not Highland at all. But then I've got a sister out in Canada, and she says out there all the pipers talk like Yanks, so where are you?

'I do everything I can to encourage a love of music,' he says. 'The first piece I'll play for you is a March, Strathspey and Reel. The March you may have heard before. It's Angus Campbell's *Farewell to Stirling* – do you know it?'

'Naw,' I says. 'We've only got one Scottish record down below and it's Sydney Devine.'

'Hm,' he says. 'It was heard a lot before the war.'

'Don't let the broken nose fool you,' I says. 'I'm only twenty-eight.'

'Well,' he says, 'the Strathspey is *Tulloch Castle* and the Reel is one I composed myself. It's called *Fiona's Reel* after my youngest daughter.'

I didn't like to ask where the daughter was. You don't like to be nosey. 'Fire away, pal,' I says.

So he played. It was great. I thought it was loud when I

heard it downstairs. But when you were right next to it, it was like sitting in a steel works.

After about five or ten minutes, getting quicker all the time, he stops. But he won't take his half of the wine, so I finish the bottle. Then I was really ready for a tune.

'C'mon, piper!' I says. 'Do you know *Amazing Grace*?'

He just ignored me. 'The next piece I will play is the Pibroch *My King Has Landed at Moydart*,' he said. 'Composed by John MacIntyre in 1745 in honour of Prince Charles Edward Stuart. Have you ever been to Glenfinnan?'

'Naw,' I says.

'Oh,' he says. 'There's a landmark there in the shape of a column, to mark the spot where the Highlanders first raised their standard, the white banner.'

'Is that right?' I says. 'Would you credit it?'

He just goes on telling me about this tune he is going to play, how it's in the Pentatonic scale of G and uses only three bars or some such – I couldn't be bothered understanding the half of it.

'This Pibroch produces a vast number of D notes,' he says.

'Well that's OK by me,' I says.

'Yes,' he says, 'but there's a natural restriction when you lift the B finger, which is quite tricky, and as a result, many pipers surreptitiously employ the use of the easier-manipulated D finger, when in competition, although whether they get away with this of course would depend on the ear and the alertness of the adjudicator.'

'Naturally,' I says. 'Do you go in for competitions yourself?'

'Not now,' he says. Then he clicks his tongue. 'The doubling on D is the real bugbear. It's been clearly defined since the days of Angus Mackay, and in every other worthwhile book of pipe music since, as a low G semiquaver, D and C demi-semiquaver followed by D. It's in perfect keeping with the other scale doublings, such as the high G and high A. But what they're getting away with now is a low G, D, low G, C, demi-semiquavers followed by D, in a kind of grip movement which to my mind sounds completely out of character with any of the other scale doublings.'

'The dirty bastards,' I says. He wasn't caring what I said, but I wasn't bothering.

'I associate this style with a crossing noise caused by dragging the C after the D gracenote,' he says. 'In fact that may have been its origin. It's not so bad when they employ it in the faster light music, but in the Pibroch, as far as I'm concerned it constitutes a definite false note and a betrayal of Scotland's whole musical tradition.'

After all that I thought we were going to get something great. But then he plays this racket that goes on for about an hour. I was fed up after about five minutes, but I didn't like to get up and walk out. So I just sat. And sat and sat and sat. Eventually he takes the chanter out of his mouth and says:

'What's the time?'

'Must be about eleven,' I says.

'Time for the news,' he says, and lays his pipes on the bed.

Well, this radio he brings out of the suitcase is about the best I've ever seen in my whole life. It's portable, battery-operated, but heavy and black and chromium plated, with built-in speakers for stereo, and it plays cassettes as well. The minute I see it I says to myself, Davie, that's for you. So we sit, and he listens to the news, and I'm hoping he'll put on a cassette after it but when the religious programme starts he stands up.

'I have to go to bed now, young man,' he says, 'I've got to get up early in the morning.'

'So have I,' I says. I didn't want him thinking I was on the buroo. 'You moving in here for good, like?'

'I've bought the place,' he says, 'to live in. It's near the University, and that's where I work.'

That's how I got to know he was a professor. 'It's not bad round here,' I says. 'I've lived here all my life. You need to watch yourself but you get a good laugh.' By this time he's opening the door for me, footering with this old Yale lock that's been fixed about ten times. 'You were done, buying this place,' I says. 'You'll not get your money back. You'll never sell it. It's all to come down.' He just smiles at me as if I'm daft. Just this weak smile, like his face'll split if he grins.

'Why should I want my money back?' he says. 'If I can live near my work rent-free for the next eight months, that'll do me fine. It was costing me a bomb where I was before. And I paid a lot less to buy this place than I did for that radio there, I can tell you. A lot less.'

I resented that smile. It was nothing, but I resented it. So as soon as he goes out the next day I come up and put in his door and grab the radio and get my mother to pawn it while I'm at my work. He doesn't smile at that.

He's down at my door as soon as I get in from work even redder than the night before. I'm all sawdust and innocence, but it never seems to cross his mind to think it could have been me. 'Davie!' he says. 'I've went and had a burglar. They kicked my door in. Splinters all over the place. Stole my good radio.'

'Is that right?' I says. 'That's terrible. So it is. Rotten. But I told you. You've got to watch round here. They're a lot of piranhas. Don't you think y'd better get the police?'

You can tell a lot about people, by asking them that question. He says really quick, 'No, no police. I don't want to be asked a lot of stupid questions. Anyway they'd never get it back now. But what about my door? Will you help me get it sorted? I've no tools. I'll make it worth your while.'

'Take your hand out of your pocket,' I says. 'I'm working with wood every day. No thief'll get through your door after I'm finished with it. And it won't cost you a penny. Just give me ten minutes to get my tea.'

He thought I was the Good Samaritan or somebody. But it was true enough what I said. It was a good job I did on that door. Made it like a fortress. Daft of me really. But that's what I did.

Not that the strongest door in the world is going to do you any good if the burglar drops in through the ceiling. That's what happens next. Other thieves have noticed that the Professor's moved in. Not just me. The day after I steal his radio two of the McGuinness boys come up. Climb through the close trap-door into the loft – you're not allowed to padlock it because of the Fire Brigade. Kick a hole in the old boy's ceiling. Jump down. Leave big mucky footprints all over the bed and make off with his bagpipes, seeing that's the only thing he's got left that's worth anything. Folk in every house in the street were laughing about it that night. But I wasn't. As far as I was concerned what they had done was a good bit over the score. To my way of thinking, the Professor's moved in beside me, okay, he's my mark. I take the best thing he's got, I'd be daft not to. But these two? Who are they? A couple of kids about seventeen that don't even come from our bit. Round the corner and half a street away, that's where they belong. They were just chancing their arm. Sneaking up like rats when they know I'm at work. A pair of chancers. And that's one thing I won't tolerate.

Not that anybody can say I don't know how to take a joke. I do. I'm not one of these headbangers you're frightened to say a word to in case they pick you up the wrong way. But at the same time, *nobody takes me for a*

mug and gets away with it. If anybody says, 'Oh, here's
Davie, let's take a loan of him' – that's when the trouble
starts. I'm not just talking about fists and feet either.
Half-bricks, broken bottles, hatchets – there's no chib I'm
afraid to use. It was a brass candlestick the time I put my
father in hospital. Fractured skull. No regrets. Take me
for a mug and you'll get a sore face for yourself, that's my
motto.

So what else can I do when I hear about the McGuinness twins, but go up that night when they're at their tea,
give the both of them a doing for poaching and hand the
Professor's pipes back to him five minutes after he gets in.
They're back in his hands before he's noticed they're
away, just about.

'You must accept some kind of reward,' he says. He
wants to give me a fiver. But the pawn's given us thirty
quid for his radio, so I knocks him back. He's that
impressed, I've got to blush, nearly.

He's even more impressed when I walks out of the close
that night and gets set upon by the McGuinness twins with
chibs, their uncle, and their uncle's pal who's over six feet
and weighs about eighteen stone. Now it's well known
that I'll fight anybody. Even if I am wee. As far as I'm
concerned it's a square go, and let the best man win. But
they come up team-handed. I'm on the deck in about five
seconds. I don't stand a chance.

My nose gets broken again. They can't kick my teeth
out. I've not had any for five years.

The Professor comes to see me in hospital, He brings
me a quarter-bottle, but I've got to just keep it. My lips
are all up like balloons.

After I come out, I can do no wrong. Two or three
week-ends running the Professor takes me about with
him. He signs me into the College Club. All chandeliers
and folk staring at you. One Saturday he hires a car, and I

get taken along too and thoroughly enjoy it. He's a birdwatcher. I've always liked sparrows and starlings and pigeons, but that day we see birds even he doesn't know the names of. Then we eat a big meal in a hotel, and take a good drink and home. He's telling me all about how he split up with his wife, by the time we get back. Me and him are real pals this one night. I'll always remember that.

But even though he's trying, the Professor can't see past the idea that, good-hearted or not, I'm still as thick as two short planks. It comes out in hundreds of ways. Very likely he never meant to do it – but it's as if every time he sees me, he's saying Poor Davie, no brains, no education, never been anywhere, Poor Davie.

Naturally I gets a bit fed up with this. That's why when I'm skint a couple of weeks before Christmas, I've got no hesitation about going up and stealing his pipes myself.

'Away up and break in,' my mother keeps saying to me. I'm off my work and me and her've been on the wine all day. Now it's about three o'clock in the afternoon and all the bottles are empty. 'Away up, son, and break in. Get something worth a few quid and we'll go down to the pawn and get the price of a few bottles. On you go.'

She's a right nagger when she's bevvied, my mother. 'Going to shut up?' I says. 'There's nothing up there worth a few quid. I told you, the place is like a bomb site.'

'There's his bagpipes,' she says. It's her that reminds me. For some reason I haven't thought of stealing them. But now I says to myself, why not? So up we go.

That's when we find out what a good job I've done on the Professor's door. I kicks my best but I'm too stoshus. I can't put it in.

'What about the trap-door the McGuinnesses got in by?' my mother says.

'He's put a good lock on it,' I says. 'Fire Brigade or not. We'll never shift that.'

'Get in by the skylight above the door then,' my mother says. She's put her finger on it. That's the only way left. So down we go for the step-ladder.

We're both that drunk we can hardly get the thing up the stair but eventually we get the step-ladder set up outside the Professor's door. 'You hold the steps,' I says, 'and I'll go up and put in the skylight.'

I've got a hammer with me, so I'm quick about it, smashing the three wee panes of glass and the two wood struts in between them. But then I've got to take my jacket off and spread it over the jaggy bottom edge that's left, so I don't cut myself when I climb over. That takes time.

'Hurry up for God's sake,' my mother's saying to me every two minutes. I starts wishing I'd left her down the stair. But at last I gets in and grabs the pipes. Then I find I can't open the door to get out. I've got rid of the Professor's old Yale lock and fitted him a nice solid mortice which of course I can't open now, seeing the key's in his pocket up at the University. So it's got to be up and over the top of the door again, only this time I'm getting held back with a pair of bagpipes up my jook and my mother the other side of the door going 'Hurry up son! Hurry up.' It gets on my nerves. It takes me all my time to hoist myself up to the top of the door.

Then we hear footsteps coming up the stair. As soon as we hear them we both know it's him. He's not supposed to be back till after five, but this day he's early. We both know it and we're right. My mother gets off her mark like a bee's stung her. She grabs the step-ladder and leaps down the stair with it, forgetting all about how it's heavy. She's trying to get it back into our house before the Professor gets that far up and sees it, fair enough. Probably she's thinking, if she can get the ladder in the house, and I can jump down quick, we might get away with it. Say we're up because we've heard suspicious noises, something like that. But I'm blazing mad all the same. I'm stuck up on top of this door like a monkey, one leg in the house and one leg out. I'm trying not to ruin myself on these wee jaggy edges. I'm totally guttered. And I've got nothing to hold on to to get myself down. I'm mad all right. Then I hears the Professor on the next landing saying hello to my mother. He's seen her with this big pair of steps in her hands coming down from his house. And his house has got a smashed-in skylight. And me right beside it. Is he going to believe me and my mother've got nothing to do with it? Even if I manage to leap down without leaving my privates eight feet up in the air? 'That's it,' I says to myself. 'The jig's up.' And I gives this wee kind of shrug, up there on top of the door, and when I do that the pipes slip out from under my jersey and fall on to the stone landing. Something breaks. From up there I can't see what.

The Professor's just arriving. He hears his pipes fall and break, but I don't think he sees them fall. I don't want to see him, anyway. I just turns my face to the wall.

He doesn't say a thing. Just picks up his bagpipes, and off down the stair and out the close. He never came back. Not as far as we know, anyway. He'd no business to have moved in, when you think about it. It wasn't as if he needed to live up our way. I don't think he was all that right in the head.

Christian Endeavour

Alan Spence

I had been a religious fanatic for only a few weeks.

'What is it the night then?' asked my father. 'The bandy hope?' I caught the mockery, but he meant no harm.

'Christian Endeavour,' I said, drying my face with a towel and stretching up to peer at myself in the cracked mirror above the sink. 'Band a Hope's on Thursday.'

The two halves of my face in the mirror didn't quite match because of the crack, were slightly out of alignment. It was an old shaving-mirror of my father's with an aluminium rim, hung squint from a nail in the window-frame.

'Ah thought Christian Endeavour was last night?'

'That was just the Juniors,' I said. 'Tonight's the Real one.'

'Are ye no too young?' said my father.

'The minister says ah can come.'

'Is that because ye were top in the bible exam?'

'Top equal,' I said. 'Ah don't know if that's why. He just said ah could come.'

'Ach well,' said my father, going back behind his newspaper. 'Keeps ye aff the streets.'

'Ah'll be the youngest there,' I said, proud of myself and wanting to share it.

'Mind yer heid in the door,' he said. 'It's that big ye'll get stuck.'

I pulled on my jacket and was ready to go.

'Seen ma bible?' I asked.

'Try lookin where ye left it,' he said.

I found it on the table with another book, *The Life of David Livingstone*, under the past week's heap of news-papers and comics. The book had been my prize in the bible exam.

The exam had been easy. Questions like *Who carried Christ's cross on the way to Calvary?* And from the Shorter Catechism, *Into what estate did the fall bring mankind?*

It was just a matter of remembering.

The label gummed in the book read FIRST PRIZE, with EQUAL penned in above BIBLE KNOWLEDGE, and then my name.

My father remembered reading the same book as a boy. He had been a sergeant in the Boys' Brigade, and the book had made him want to be a missionary himself.

'Great White Doctor an that,' he said. 'Off tae darkest Africa.'

But somehow he had drifted away from it all. 'Wound up in darkest Govan instead,' he said.

For the years he had been in the Boys' Brigade, he had been given a long-service badge. I still kept it in a drawer with a hoard of other badges I had gathered over the years. Most of them were cheap tin things, button badges: ABC Minors, Keep Britain Tidy. But the BB badge was special, heavier metal in the shape of an anchor. I had polished it with Brasso till it shone. There were two other treasures in the drawer: an army badge an uncle had given me, shaped like a flame, and a Rangers supporters badge, a silver shield with the lion rampant in red.

Christian Endeavour had a badge of its own. A dark blue circle with a gold rim, and CE in gold letters. The Sunday-school teachers at the Mission all wore it. I had been disappointed that there wasn't one for the Juniors. But now that I was moving up, I would be entitled to wear the badge. CE. In gold.

'Is ther gonnae be any other youngsters there the night?' asked my father.

'Jist Norman,' I said. Norman was the minister's son. He was twelve, a year older than me.

'Ye don't like him, do ye?'

'He's a big snotter,' I said. 'Thinks e's great.'

'Wis he top in the bible exam as well?'

'Top equal,' I said. My father laughed.

'That minister's quite a nice wee fella,' he said. 'That time he came up here, after yer mother died, we had quite a wee chat.'

'Aye, ye told me,' I said.

'Ah think he got a surprise. Wi me no goin tae church an that, he musta thought ah was a bitty a heathen. Expected tae find me aw bitter, crackin up y'know.'

'Aye, ah know.'

'But ah wisnae. Ah showed um ma long-service badge fae the BB. Even quoted scripture at him!'

'Aye.'

'"In my father's house there are many mansions" ah said. That's the text they read at the funeral.'

'Time ah was going,' I said.

'He wanted me tae come tae church,' said my father. 'But ah cannae be bothered wi aw that. Anywey, you're goin enough for the two ae us these days, eh?'

'Aye. Cheerio, da.'

'See ye after, son.'

I took a last look at my reflection in the squinty mirror.

'Right,' I said.

I took the shortcut to the Mission, across the back courts. It was already dark, and in the light from the windows I could make out five or six boys in the distance. From their noise I could recognize them as my friends, and I hurried on, not really wanting them to see me. If they asked where I was going, they would only mock.

I hadn't been out with them this week, except for playing football after school. They thought I was soft in the head for going so much to the Mission. They couldn't understand. I felt a glow. It was good to feel good. It had come on stronger since my mother had died. The Mission was a refuge from the empty feeling of lack.

But part of me was always drawn back to my friends, to their rampaging and their madness.

I heard a midden-bin being overturned, a bottle being smashed, and the gang of boys scattered laughing through the backs as somebody shouted after them from a third-storey window. Head down, I hurried through a close and out into the street.

Now that I was almost at the Mission, I felt nervous and a little afraid. I had never been to an adult meeting before. I thought of the lapel-badge with the gold letters. CE. Perhaps I would even be given one tonight. Initiated. There was another badge I had seen the teachers wearing. It was green with a gold lamp, an oil lamp like Aladdin's. But maybe that was only for ministers and teachers.

Give me oil in my lamp, keep me burning.
Give me oil in my lamp I pray,
Halleluja!

The Mission hall was an old converted shop, the windows covered over with corrugated iron. A handwritten sign on the door read CHRISTIAN ENDEAVOUR. Tonight. 7.30. I stood for a moment, hesitating, outside. Then I pushed open the door and went in to the brightness and warmth.

I was early, and only a handful of people had arrived. They sat, talking, in a group near the front of the hall, and nobody seemed to have noticed me come in.

Norman was busy stacking hymn-books. Looking up, he saw me and nodded, then went out into the back room.

The minister saw me then and waved me over. There were two or three earnest conversations going on. The minister introduced me to a middle-aged African couple.

'These are our very special guests,' he said. 'Mr and Mrs Lutula.'

'How do you do,' we all said, and very formally shook hands. There was a momentary lull then the conversations picked up again. But I could feel the big black woman looking at me.

'And tell me,' she said, her voice deep like a man's, 'when did the Lord Jesus come into your heart?'

'Pardon?' I said, terrified.

'Ah said, when did the Lord Jesus come into your heart, child?'

That was what I thought she had said. And she wanted an answer. From me. I looked up at the broad face smiling at me, the dark eyes shining. I looked down at the floor. I could feel myself blush. What kind of question was that to ask? How was I supposed to answer it?

Why didn't she ask me something straightforward?
Who carried Christ's cross on the way to Calvary?
Joseph of Aramathea.
Into what estate did the fall bring mankind?
The fall brought mankind into an estate of sin and misery.

I sat, tense and rigid, on the hard wooden seat. Now my face was really hot and flushed. I cleared my throat. In a squeak of a voice I said, 'I don't know if . . .'

I look at the floor.

She leaned over and patted my arm. 'Bless you, child,' she said, smiling, and turned to talk to her husband.

I stood up, still looking at the floor. I made my way, conscious of every step, clumsy and awkward, to the back of the hall and out into the street. I walked faster; I began to run, away from the Mission, along the street, through the close into the back court.

The night air cooled me. I stopped and leaned against a midden wall. I was in absolute misery, tortured by my own sense of foolishness. It wasn't just the question, it was what it had opened up; a realm where I knew nothing, could say nothing.

When did the Lord Jesus come into my heart? I could have said it was when my mother died. That would have sounded pious. But I didn't think it was true. I didn't know. That was it; I didn't know. If the Lord Jesus had come into my heart, I should know.

And how could I go back in now? It was all too much for me. I would tell the minister on Sunday I had felt hot and flushed, had gone outside for some air. That much was true. I would say I had felt sick and gone home.

The back court was quiet. There was no sound, except for the TV from this house or that. Bright lit windows in the dark tenement blocks. I walked on, slow, across the back, and as I passed another midden, I kicked over a bin, and ran.

Nearer home I slowed down again.

My father would ask why I was back so early.

The Time Keeper

Elspeth Davie

It was taken as a matter of course that at one time or other during the summer he would be showing people around his city. Renwick was a hospitable man and for certain weeks it was a duty to be available to visitors. The beauty of the place was written on its skyline in a sharp, black script of spires, chimneys and turrets and in the flowing line of a long crag and hill. It was written up in books. He had shelves devoted to its history and its architecture. It was written on anti-litter slogans with the stern injunction that this was a beautiful city and it had better be kept that way.

Sometimes the people he took on were those wished on him for an hour or two, friends of friends, or persons he'd met by chance passing through on their way north. They were all sightseers of a sort and the first sight they wanted to see, particularly if they were foreigners, was himself. Well, he was on the spot of course. Yes, he had to admit he probably *was* a sight and even worth looking at in a very superficial way. At certain times he put on his advocate's garb – a highly stylized get-up, dark, narrow and formal. A bowler hat went with the suit and an umbrella which – because of the windiness of the city – often remained unrolled. He was never solemn about the business. He was the first to point out that it was traditional wear – a kind of fancy dress or disguise. 'And there are plenty of them about these days,' he would say. 'We ourselves are falling behind in the game. Look at all the

people either dressing the part or the opposite of the part!'
But there was no need of excuse. Visitors enjoyed him in
his dress and were disappointed to discover he seldom
wore it when the Court was not sitting. Sometimes
however they were lucky. And he had a face that went
with the garb – a rather masked face, long and grave with
hair well plastered down over a neat skull as though to
show what an extreme of flatness could be achieved in
comparison with the dashing wig which he might later put
on.

Renwick's hospitality didn't mean that he was always a
patient man. There was a good deal of exasperation and
sharpness in his character, and he shared with many of his
fellow citizens a highly argumentative and sceptical turn of
mind. He developed it and was valued for it. That hint of
the suspicious Scot in his make-up was well hidden. The
impatience was not so well in check. It boiled up silently at
dullness. It occasionally exploded at stupidity. As time
went on he had even begun to be impatient with those
visitors who insisted on taking a purely romantic view of
the city. It was not, after all, made up only of interesting
stones, nor were the people going about their business on
top of these stones particularly romantic. Certainly not.
They were a common-sense, very businesslike lot and
more to be compared to down-to-earth scene-shifters
doing their jobs against a theatrical background.

This was made clear to an American couple one afternoon as they stood with him in one of the oldest
graveyards of the city. There was a great deal to see and a
lot to hear about. Renwick had given them something of
the turbulent history of the place and listed the succession
of famous persons who had been buried here. They in
their turn exclaimed about the ancient monuments and
walls. They touched the moss-covered dates on head-
stones. It was getting late. The three or four still left in the

place were slowly making their way out. In the distance a blonde girl was moving round the dark church between black and white tombstones. But Renwick's couple were all for lingering in the place until the sun went down. Renwick felt a sudden flare of impatience rise inside him. He directed them to look up and out of the place. From where they stood they could see, rising on all sides, the backs of houses and churches, and beyond that a glimpse of the bridge which carried a busy street over a chasm. Cars and buses crossed it. People went striding past. 'But look up there,' he said pointing. 'We are rather an energetic crowd. You can see we're in a hurry. You're not going to find your ordinary citizen of the place sitting around staring at old stones for long. I believe you might find it hard enough to get him to stop and talk for any length of time unless there was very good reason for it. For better or worse – that is our character!'

The Americans didn't deny this. They had already attempted to detain people on the bridge. They had sensed the bracing air. Now, polite but silent, they stared down at an angel whose round and rather sulky face was crowned by a neat, green crewcut of moss and backed by frilly wings sprouting behind his ears. Cautiously they mentioned the old ghosts of the place. 'But just behind you,' came the brisk voice, 'there in that wall, there are still lived-in houses. Look at that window for instance.' It was true that in the actual ancient wall of the place they were looking into the room of a house. Sitting in the open window was an old man being shaved by someone standing behind. At first they saw only a hand holding his chin, the other hand drawing a razor along his cheek. But while they watched the job was done. The head of the old man and his middle-aged daughter emerged from the window. It was close enough to get a clear sight of them – keen, unsmiling, both staring down with eyes which were shrewd but without much curiosity, as though they had seen decades of tourists standing just below them there on that particular spot in the churchyard.

'You see there are more than just angels around us,' said Renwick tersely. 'There are also ordinary, busy folk getting on with their own jobs.' The young couple looked for a moment as though they might question the busyness and even the ordinariness, but had thought better of it, especially as they had seen Renwick look openly at his wrist.

Renwick counted himself a polite man. Lately, however, he had given in to this habit, common to persons of consequence in the city, of glancing at his watch – and often while people were actually talking to him. He believed that he was indicating in the politest possible way that he was a very busy man, that even in summer his time was limited. But as the habit grew not only visitors but even friends began to see the wrist shoot out, no longer surreptitiously but very openly. Those who still hung around after that had only themselves to blame. And as well as the watch he was very well up in the tactics of the engagement diary. 'Well, certainly not tomorrow, nor the day after. This week's out in fact. Next week? Full up, I'm afraid. No, I have a space here. I think I can *just* about manage to fit you in.' Acquaintances might sound grateful but they felt squeezed and sometimes throttled as they watched him writing them into the minimal space between appointments.

Just as Renwick was proud and yet irritated by the romantic reputation of the city, so he felt about the supernatural history of the place. He was good-natured about disguises, masks of all kinds. He understood the hidden. But the guise of the supernatural he didn't care for. He had lost count of the number of times he was asked about the witches and warlocks of the city, medieval apparitions hidden down closes, the eighteenth-century ghosts of the New Town. Grudgingly he pointed to deserted windows where heads had looked out and stairs where persons without their heads had walked down. Reluctantly he led willing visitors to the district where the major had made his pact, pointed out infamous tenements and doorways blasted with the Devil's curse. 'And now you'll want to see the spot where the gallows stood – and you'll not mind if I leave you there. I have to keep an eye on my time. The fact is I have a good deal of business to attend to between now and supper.'

Friends dated his concern with time back to a year when his post brought new responsibilities. Others pointed out that busyness was all a matter of choice and that the time-obsession was common to most middle-aged men once they'd begun to feel it making up on them. 'And worse things can happen to a man than working to a tight schedule,' remarked a colleague as they discussed others in the profession. 'We've had a good few suicides by his age, and quite a tearing of the silk. There was McInnes letting it all rip and making off for the South Seas. And Webster? Wasn't it the stage he'd always yearned for, never the Bar? Yes, retired now, white hair to the shoulders – happy enough they say, and no guile in the man at all. Still, meeting him late on summer nights in loopy hats with orange feathers gave some people more of a turn than seeing the Devil himself.' Other names came up. They decided if it was nothing more than a little touchiness about time – Renwick was doing well enough.

By midsummer a stream of holiday-makers were on the streets. Renwick would become impatient – or was it envious? – at the idea of an endless enjoyment of leisure. How could they wander for days and weeks, sometimes for months? From early spring when the first few aimless visitors arrived he would begin to take note of the city clocks. Not that he hadn't known them all his life – the clocks under church spires, the clocks on schools and hospitals and church towers. He'd seen brand-new timepieces erected in his day and had attended the unveilings of memorial clocks. But now he counted them as allies in the summer game, to give him backing when the wristwatch methods had no result. It was his habit, then, to stare about him for the nearest clock – if it was old so much the better. Having alerted visitors to its history it was an easy step to exclaim at the time of day, to excuse himself and make off at all possible speed to the next appointment.

During one summer Renwick had several visitors of his own for a short time. He enjoyed their stay. They knew the city well. It was not always necessary to accompany them, but he had the pleasure of their talk in the evening. Later, however, he was asked if he would help a friend out with four visitors who had been staying in the city and, with little warning, were to land on him for twelve hours. The friend had to be out of town on the evening of that day. Could Renwick possibly take them round for half an hour or so? Yes, he could do that. When the time came they turned out to be two middle-aged couples from the south who had not set foot in the city before this visit. But they had read the necessary books. They were well primed with history and they knew legends about every door and windowframe. They had expected smoky sunsets and they got them. They knew that on certain nights there might be a moon directly above the floodlit castle. The moon was in the prescribed spot the first night they'd arrived. They did not mind bad weather. They said that gloom and darkness suited the place. They liked the mist and even the chill haar that could swirl up out of the sea after a warm day. They were amiable and they had an equal and unqualified love for all the figures in the city's past.

That evening Renwick had taken them down into one of the closes of the Lawnmarket and they were now standing in a large court enclosed by tenement walls. There were a few people besides themselves in the place – a group of youths with bottles bulging at their hips, a fair-haired girl holding a guidebook and three small children who had rushed in after a ball and out again. It was getting late and a few small yellow lights were showing high up on the surrounding walls.

'If only we could get in and see some of those weird old rooms,' said one of the wives, staring up.

'And speak to one or two of the old folk,' her husband added. 'There'll be ones up there with many a tale to tell of the old days.'

'Many a tale?' Renwick straightened his shoulders. He directed a rather chilly smile over the heads of the group. 'No doubt there might be tales – and ones not so very different from our own. Of course those particular rooms you're looking at have all been re-done. They are expensive places, very well equipped, I should imagine, with all the latest gadgets. You'll find quite young, very well set-up persons living there, I believe. You'll get your dank walls, poor drains, black corners in a good many other places if you care to look. But not up there!'

They had been with him now for half an hour. Renwick had begun to check the various times on their watches with his own, and murmuring: 'I will just make sure,' had walked down the few steps at the far end of the court and out to where, overlooking street and gardens, he could see the large, lit clock at the east end of the city. 'I must be off in five minutes,' he said when he came back, '. . . letters to attend to . . . a paper to prepare . . .' They asked if he could give them an idea what they should look at the following morning. Briefly he outlined a plan and described the things they should see. They asked if they would meet him again. He explained that he might or might not meet them in a couple of days depending on his work. 'Do you work all through the holidays?' someone innocently asked. Renwick made a non-committal gesture to the sky. At the same time he noticed that the fair-haired girl who'd been wandering about for some time between their group and the shadowy end of the court, had come forward and now stood with them directly under the lamp. Stunning. Not nowadays a word he was in the habit of using. But what other word for this particular kind of fairness? Straight white-blonde hair, fair eyebrows against brown skin, and eyes so pale they had scarcely more colour than water. A Scandinavian – the intonation was clear in a few words she spoke to one of the women, but she was also that idealized version which – along with its opposite – each country holds of another part of the world – strikingly tall, strong and fair – and no doubt outspoken. Renwick waited for her to speak. She lifted her arm with the back of her wrist towards him. She tapped her watch. 'You have given us your minutes. Exactly five. Your time is up,' she said. The others laughed. Renwick smiled. So she had seen his clock-watching, heard his work programme, had simply stopped in passing for a laugh. But attention was now turned her way. They were asking questions. And it appeared that in her country the light was different. The sun, they gathered, was very bright, the darkness more intense. Different, she made it plain, though not of course better. They took it in, unblinking, while they stared. It seemed they got the message on light in a single flash and with no trouble at all. The girl left the place soon afterwards and to Renwick it seemed that his two couples were slowly merged together again, and he with them – all welded into the state called middle-age. No amount of good sense, God-given wisdom or hard-won experience, and least,

least of all the beauties of maturity were ever going to mend this matter. There they were. Some light had left them.

One way or another this was to occupy him a good deal during the next day. It was not just that at some stage of life the optimstic beam had been replaced by a smaller light, but that from the start even his awareness of actual physical light had been limited. It was hard for him to imagine variations – how some lights sharpened every object and its shadow for miles around while others made a featureless flatness of the same scene. He tried to imagine those regions of the world made barren to the bone by sun, and others soaked by the same sun to make ground and water prosper from one good year to the next. He thought with relief of white cornfields nearer home and imagined with a shock of hope streams so transparent you could see the fish, leaves and stones shining in their depths.

The phone drilled at his skull. 'Tomorrow evening – would it be possible for half an hour if you can manage to spare the time?' Both couples were leaving the next morning. Yes, it would be just possible to fit it in. They would meet at the bottom of the street leading from Palace to Castle. They would walk slowly up. Another voice joined the first in thanking him.

'The weather has been disappointing for you today,' said Renwick as he waited for the moment to put the phone down.

'No, this is how we like it,' came the reply. 'Clear, sharp, with a touch of frost.' This might pass with those who knew him as a rough description of himself. Or not so rough. Exact perhaps – though some might put the complimentary touch, others a hatching of black lines. Renwick said he was glad to hear it and replaced the receiver thoughtfully.

The next evening was overcast with a slight wind which sent the black and white clouds slowly across the sky. They were waiting for him eagerly. 'A disappointing evening,' he said as if to test them again. On the contrary they were enthusiastic. This was the city at its best, at its most characteristic. Renwick saved his disappointment for himself. They walked slowly up, going in and out of closes, through doors and arches. They saw the sea through openings and climbed halfway up stairways worn into deep curves. Renwick led the way through the darker wynds. He answered questions. Apart from this he said little. The street grew steep, crossed a main road and went on up until it opened out to the broad space in front of the church of St Giles with the Law Courts behind. It was growing dark and from this rise where they were standing they could see down almost the whole length of the street illumined by blue street lights. It was a favourite viewing point for tourist buses and their guides and there were still a few about. People were roaming around the precincts of the Courts and going to and from the church.

Renwick looked round and stared pointedly at the large, lit clock of the Tolbooth, big as a harvest moon. Further down the street were smaller clocks. Automatically following his eyes, the others stared too. They got the message. Time was important even to citizens of an historic city. Things must move on. Turning back again Renwick saw the blonde girl a few steps away. She had been looking at the church. Now she was making a beeline for his group. So he had been watched again, scrutinized no doubt as an exhibit of the place, one worth remembering perhaps, but remembered with a good deal more amusement than respect. She had reached the group now and stood waiting until the couples wandered off to make the most of their last minutes of sight-seeing – then she remarked: 'You have very few angels inside. I have seen the churches. Some of them are very beautiful and very bare.'

'You're absolutely right,' said Renwick. He lectured her gently on the reasons for it. 'Any angels we do have are mostly outside,' he added, – 'hidden away in cemeteries.' And if it came to angels it was true enough the blue light had given her own face a marbly shine, her hair a touch of green. But her eyes had neither the exalted nor the downcast look of churchyard angels. They were too direct, too challenging for an angel's eyes. She was not the kind to be hidden away. He was going on to an explanation of the spot where they were standing when something struck him. 'I am not a guide,' said Renwick.

'Well I think you are,' said the young woman. 'You keep them all together. You keep the time. That is important – how you keep the time. Clocks are important, very important indeed. Clocks are – how do you say? – they are very much up your street.' Saying this, she made a quick survey of the street from top to bottom as he had done some minutes before. Her performance managed, miraculously, to be both amiable and derisive. She made way genially for the others when they came back and after some talk with them went off again.

There was nothing to take him out the following evening. Nobody demanded his time. Yet the next night after supper he was out trudging up the High Street again. The place was still crowded and he made his way around groups at corners and through lines of people who were spread out across the width of the street. This time he felt the need to look about him with the eye of a stranger. Many times he stopped to stare at familiar things and once in a while, as if from the corner of his eye, managed to catch some object by surprise. It was a warm night. Far above him he saw rows of elbows upon windowsills and shadowy heads staring down, and above the heads a rocky outline of roofs and steep, black gable walls blocking the night sky. Sometimes he turned back for a closer look at the scrolls or archways or to search for some small stone head over a door. He had become a tourist among tourists, staring at persons and buildings – critical, admiring, sometimes bored, sometimes amazed at what he saw. He grew tired. His own feet looked strange to him as he stepped on and off the kerb or dodged the slippery stones on uneven bits of pavement. He plodded on. His face confronted him, unawares, in dark shop windows, and different from the conscious face in the bedroom mirror. This person looked distraught, looked lonely, battered even, and hardly to be distinguished from some of the down-and-outs who wandered in and out of nearby pubs.

Renwick had come a long way. The Castle was now in view and it was giving all of them the full treatment. He had seen this often enough – illumined stone and black battlements against a sky still red with sunset. To crown all – a huge, white supermoon breaking through clouds. Renwick found himself in the midst of a large group, all turned that way, all staring as if at a high stage. They were a long time staring. Suddenly, as if at a warning buzz in the brain, Renwick resumed citizenship. He was proud yet impatient of the wide eyes around him. He glanced at his watch, heard his own voice repeat familiar words:

'Yes, that's how it is – very dramatic, very spectacular. Illumined? Yes, very often. The full moon? Yes, don't ask me how – it *seems* often to be full and very well placed, though more romantically speaking than astronomically I would say. You must remember though – we are not only a romantic city. Far from it. Yes, yes, of course there's stuff coming down, but have you seen the new things going up – the business side of things? In other words we are a *busy* people. Time moves on, you see. It moves on here as in every other place.' He looked a man of some consequence, a very busy man with a full timetable to get through. They made way for him. He wished them good-night, passed on.

He was alone now and walking in a quiet side street. The moon and the red sky were behind, the illumination blocked out by high office buildings. He was making for home. Once he stopped in passing for a word with an acquaintance, until they reminded one another of the time and quickly separated. Five persons made up on him and passed, talking animatedly, and Renwick recognized the cadence of this tongue. The blonde girl was walking with three others and a young man. The man was native to the city. The rest, he noted, were all tall, all fair, all dressed with a flare and colour that stood out even in the dark street. If this was the northern myth it was coming over in style. The girl gave him a wave as they went by.

'A fine night,' said Renwick.

'Yes,' the girl called back. 'And how about your moon tonight? Have you looked yet? Has it turned into a clock?' He heard her answering the young man, heard her say in a voice – low, but audible to touchy ears: 'No, no, not moonstruck. He is a time keeper. The man is clock-mad!' She made some remark to the others in her own language. They laughed, looked back over their shoulders and gave him a friendly wave. All five went on their way, noiseless, in rubber soles, and disappeared round the next corner.

But Renwick's shoes were loud on the paving-stones, the footsteps rang in his ears like a metronome. But what were they counting out? Minutes or stones? He stared round once, then turned his back again. This moon had looked cold and white as a snowball. Yet his moonlit ears burned as he walked on.

The Hitch-Hiker

James Kelman

It was a terrible night. From where we were passing the loch lay hidden in the heavy rain and in the mist, the mist had come suddenly. We followed the bend leading around and down towards the village. Each of us held an empty box above his head; the barman had given them to us and they were saturated but better than nothing. We trudged in silence. When we arrived at the bridge over the burn, Chic said: There's a hitch-hiker.

She was standing at the gate entrance to one of the small cottages. She appeared to be hesitating. But she went on in, and chapped at the door. The light came on inside and a woman answered, she shook her head and pointed along the road. The three of us were now passing by the cottage. Thirty yards on I turned back to look, in time to see her entering another gate. A man answered the call this time but shut the door almost immediately, the bastard. The girl was standing there staring up at the window above the door; the porchlight went off. Two large rucksacks strapped on to her back and shoulders, and when she walked from the door she seemed bent under their weight. Old Rooney grunted. Young lassie like that, he said. She shouldnt be out walking on a night like this.

Aye, said Chic. Doesnt look as if she's anywhere to go but.

I nodded. Drenched as well. Look at her.

Well she's not the only one, son, said Old Rooney. Come on.

Just a minute, I said.

The girl had noticed us standing watching her; she quickened her pace a bit, in the opposite direction. The old man said: She's feart.

What . . .

He grinned as he indicated the state we were in, the cardboard boxes and working gear and so on. What d'you expect with us staring at her? He paused, If she was my lassie . . . She shouldn't be out on a night like this!

Not her fault she cant get a lift or a place to kip.

Old Rooney glanced at me: Single lassies shouldnt go hitching on their tod.

The auld yin's right, laughed Chic, not with bastards like us going about.

Come on, said the old man. Catch pneumonia hanging around in this weather.

Just a minute, wait till we see what happens.

Rooney glowered at me, grunted under his breath and spat into the ditch. The girl was chapping on the next door by this time. The person who answered gestured along in our direction. But once the door closed she gazed at us then carried on in the opposite way. I said, That's bad that – not letting her in.

Chic laughed: I'd let her in in a minute.

Away you ya manky soinso, cried old Rooney. He stopped, raised his eyebrows and grinned. Still, he said, not a bad wee bum on her.

They specs of yours auld yin, they must have x-ray lenses to see through that anorak she's wearing.

When you get to my age son . . .

Bet you she's a foreigner, said Chic. Eh?

I nodded. A certainty.

The girl had almost disappeared into the mist. She crossed over the bridge then, and was gone. Right, said Rooney. I'm off.

Might as well, agreed Chic.

The two of them walked on; I strode after them a moment later. Auld yin, I said. Can she stay the night with us?

Don't be daft, son.

How not?

No room.

Plenty room.

Jesus Christ, son, he said, sharing a caravan with the three of us? Are you kidding? Anyway – the lassie herself would never wear it.

I'll go and ask her. Tell her it's okay. She can have my bunk. I'll kip on the floor.

Rooney looked at me and then at the other and he said: What do you say Chic?

Chic shrugged.

Good on you, Chick, I said.

Rooney shook his head, he spat into the ditch again and muttered, Goodsafuckingmaritans.

Thanks auld yin.

She'll never wear it, he called after me.

When I saw her I slowed down. She had stopped to shrug the rucksacks up on to her shoulders in a more comfortable position. A few paces on and she halted again. I caught up to her and said: Hullo. But the girl ignored me, continued walking on beneath the weight. I said another hullo and she halted suddenly. To see me she had to turn her body side on to me. And she was raging. Glaring at me. In a moment I said: Have you no place to stay?

Hoisting the rucksacks up again she about-turned and went off as fast as she could. I went on after her. She was incredibly angry. And before I managed to get my mouth opened she stopped to yell: WHAT?

Have you not got a place for the night?

Pardon . . . She was not really asking me to repeat it, but seemed to be playing for time; glancing up and down the road. Nobody in sight. Never anybody in sight in this place, not even in a heatwave; out in the middle of the wilds it was with nothing bar a village and a hotel close by.

Dont worry, I said to her. You need a house for the night. A place out the rain, eh?

What?

A house.

You know? she said.

Hotel, there's a hotel.

Ah. Yes yes yes hotel. Hotel, she shrugged, much money. She glanced at me and added, Please – I go.

Listen a minute. You can come to our place. I have place.

I . . . do not understand.

You can come to our place. It's okay. A caravan. Better than hanging about here catching a cold.

She pointed at my chest. You stay?

Aye. Yes, I stay. Caravan.

No.

And off she trudged. I caught up with her again. Look, I said, it's okay. No bother. Not just me. Two mates. Three of us here. It isnt . . . it's okay. It will be alright. Honest.

She turned on me. Raging again. What a face. She cried, One two three. And she counted out three fingers. One two three, all man and me. Tapping a finger to her temples she went on her way without hesitation. At the lane that leads up to the modern cottages where the forestry workers lived, the girl paused for a second then continued along and out of sight.

Inside the caravan Chic had opened me a can of lager while I finished drying off my hair. Both he and old

Rooney were already under the blankets. They were sitting up as they sipped from the cans and smoked their cigarettes. The rain was battering off the sides and the roof and the windows of the caravan. Chic was saying: But did you manage to get through to her?

What d'you mean did I manage to get through to her! Course I didnt get through to her. Thought I was about to rape her or something.

Rooney laughed, Hell of a blow that to your ego son, eh?

Fuck my ego. Tell you one thing auld yin – I'll not sleep the night.

Aye you will, said Chic grinning. You get used to it.

You never get used to it. Rooney said: Never mind but. You can have a chug when we're away to sleep.

The old man laid his can of beer on the floor to light another cigarette from the burning end of his old one. He began chuckling to himself. He glanced at us, he said: Mind fine when I was at Doncaster . . .

Hell with Doncaster, I cried.

Chic laughed: Never mind him auld yin. Let's hear it.

Old Rooney smiled. No Chic, wouldnt be fair to the boy here.

When I had dried my feet I walked into the kitchenette to hang up my towel. The top section of the window was open, I closed it. The rain was as heavy but the mist was thinning. She'll be swimming out there, said Chic on my return. I nodded and sat down on my bunk with the can of lager.

Aye, said the old man. Pity you never thought to tell her about next door, son!

I stared around at him.

The sparks, he continued, they wont be back for a day or so. Had to go back down the road for something.

Jesus Christ, I said: Are you kidding?

He started laughing.

Nothing funny about it ya bad auld bastard, I said.

I forgot, he said spluttering, honest son. I forgot all about it.

Forgot, by Christ!

Chic also began laughing.

Fine pair of mates this, I said. Never have signed on in the first place if I'd known about yous two pair of bastarn comedians. Eh? No wonder they keep dumping yous out into the wilds to work.

Will you listen to this boy, cried Rooney. He was hysterical, went into a paroxysm of coughing.

Keeping to the side of the track I walked quickly along it from the small group of caravans. The centre of the track was bogging. It was always bogging. Even during the hot recent dry spell it had been bogging, and plastered in animal shit. Hopeless attempting to keep from sliding down into the worst of it. By the time I reached the road my boots and the bottoms of my jeans were in a hell of a mess. I headed back along to the village. A few cottages and a nearby hotel and the bastards called it a village.

It was black until I approached them, then an occasional porchlight lighted my way. The mist had almost disappeared completely. I walked up the lane to the modern cottages but no sight of her. I was peering into each garden. If she was around here she was sheltering in somewhere. I returned to the road and headed around the bend in the road towards the hotel. The rain had lessened, I could see moonlight reflecting on the waters of the loch a distance out; close in it was black.

At the wall next the car-park entrance she was standing, just to the side of the hotel. Talking to this very old man who was wearing a complete outfit of yellow oilskins. A dog stood panting at his heels. He was talking with her in

French. My approach had been noted; he watched me come forwards. The girl finished by muttering something to him, and he nodded. She made a movement of some kind, her face tightened; she looked in the direction of the loch.

Has she got a place yet?

What was that? he said looking away from me.

A place. Has she got a place yet? She was looking for a place for the night.

Oh. A place.

Aye, I said.

The old fellow regarded me then he shook his head. I was telling her to try up at Missus McLeod's house.

Were you?

Aye. I was telling her to try it there. You know Missus McLeod, I would think?

No. I dont know her at all.

Aye, you wouldnt know her house then. Eh. No, I dont think she'll be having any rooms at this time of night. Missus McLeod . . . He shook his head. A queer woman that yin.

The girl was now gazing in through the car-park entrance, but her gaze had included me in the manoeuvre. Look, I said to the old fellow, I'm living down in the caravan site. There's one empty next to mine. Some workmen ɪat were using it have had to get back to Glasgow for a while. Tell her she's welcome to it for the night.

He looked at me.

She'll be on her tod, I said, I'm not up to anything. Just tell her that.

I glanced at her as he began speaking to her until eventually she nodded. He added something to which she again nodded. He said to me: She'll go.

I told him to tell her to let me carry her rucksacks. She

shook her head, the old fellow shrugged. Both of us watched her hitching them up onto her shoulders. Then she spoke very seriously to him and he smiled, and he patted her arm.

And she was off.

She stared directly to the front of her thick hiking boots. We passed over the bridge and on in silence to the turnoff for the site. The rain began falling more heavily, although the mist had evaporated. She stopped and shrugged up the rucksacks. A rumble from the mountains across the loch was followed by a strike of lightning which brightened the length of the track for a moment. A crack of thunder. Look, I said indicating the rucksacks and the bogging path, I better get a hold of your stuff. I helped them from her. She swung them around and down, and I put one over each of my shoulders. Setting off along the grass verge on the inside, at the thick bushes, I heard her come splashing through the centre of the track at my rear, not bothering at all, just splashing through it. The light was out in our caravan. Indicating it I pointed to my chest and then indicated the one adjacent. Yours, I said. I opened it up for her, stood back to let her enter but she waved me in first. I dumped the rucksacks on the kitchenette floor and opened the door in to the room. It was only a two-berth. A stale smell of sweaty socks clouded the place, but it was fairly tidy. The girl had her arms folded and her shoulders hunched up as if she had recently shivered; she was standing with her back to the built-in wardrobe. I nodded. Be back in a minute, I said.

In the dark interior of our caravan I saw the red glow from old Rooney's cigarette. Chic was snoring slightly. I heard you coming, said the old man.

Any tea-bags?

Take a look in my coat pockets.

I also collected the tin of condensed milk and washed out two mugs. Teeming down out there, I said.

Aye.

She's soaked to the skin. I hesitated before leaving, added: Good night, auld yin.

Good night, son.

I chapped on the door and went in. She was sitting on a bunk, but still wearing the anorak, and her boots. Her hands were thrust deep into the anorak pockets. When I had the water boiling and poured, I passed her a mugful of tea. She held it in both hands for a while. I said, No food.

Pardon?

Food. I've got no food.

Ah. And she put the tea down on the floor and drawing across a rucksack, she opened it up and withdrew a plastic container from which she handed me up a sandwich. She closed the container without taking one for herself, picked up the tea and held it between her hands again. I had not wanted a sandwich either, but I ate it anyway. A few sips of the tea and she said: Tea is good.

Cant beat it.

She glanced at me and I shrugged, Tea is good.

Yes, she said.

She refused a cigarette and once I had lighted my own, said: You work?

Aye, yes.

Not stay, she said gesturing outside the window. Rain was pounding down out there.

No, I said. Not stay here, thank Christ. Glasgow I stay in.

Ah, she nodded. My friend also is Glasgow.

Great place Glasgow, eh?

Glasgow very good.

Have another drop of splosh.

Pardon?

More tea?

She shook her head. No. You . . . ah . . . you, ah . . .
She paused then went on in French and giving me a look
she shrugged, but half smiled. I cannot say . . .

I shrugged as well.

You go now, she said.

I go now.

Yes, she nodded.

In the morning I shall be here.

Tired tired tired, she smiled. You go now.

I go now.

Both of them had washed and were ready to leave. When
old Rooney entered the kitchenette to rinse out the mugs I
said: Hey Chic, think the auld yin'll mind if I'm late in this
morning?

Ask him and see, he replied.

Rooney scratched his chin when I did ask but he said,
Okay. Dont be all morning but.

I tugged the sheet up to my neck. As soon as they had
gone I got up out of the bunk and dressed, brushed my
teeth, shaved. Outside it was fresh, dry: a clear open
morning with puffy white clouds about the mountains. In
the hotel bar the previous night, old Rooney had forecast
a return of the hot weather; it looked as if he was going to
be correct once again.

No reply when I chapped on the caravan door. I
chapped again and went inside. Clothes were strewn
around the interior, she appeared to have unpacked every
last item. Her smell was here. She was sleeping. Her
breathing short, regular; lying on her side facing into the
wall. I retreated. Outside I pulled the door closed quietly
then chapped it loudly. I heard rustling. I clicked open the
door.

No.

It's me.

No.

I remained on the outside step with my hand on the knob.

Come.

Her hair was rumpled. A pair of jeans and a tee shirt she was wearing, her eyes sleepy and half shut. She began moving about picking things up from the floor and folding them together and sticking them back into the rucksacks, but there was so much stuff lying around it seemed unlikely she could get everything back in. I went into the kitchenette, filled the kettle and shoved it on the stove.

Tea! she called.

Aye. Yes, tea.

Your friends?

Work.

Ah.

She stopped straightening things out and with a yawn she sat down on the bunk with her back against the wall and her legs drawn up, resting her elbows on her knees. Looking out of the window over her shoulder she murmured something in her own language and tossed her hair. I said: Sleep?

She nodded. Good.

She reached down and brought out the plastic container, gave me a sandwich as I gave her a mugful of tea. I sat on the other bunk. It's a good morning, I said to her.

You . . . ah, you . . . ah, she stopped and finished it in French. We both shrugged.

Tea good?

Tea very, very good, she said smiling. She pointed to the plastic container and I nodded. She gave me another

sandwich. She laughed, In Glasgow . . . she held up her
sandwich . . . In Glasgow a piece, yes? My friend say
geeza piece please.

That's right, I said. More tea?

Little.

In less than an hour she was set. I helped her heave the
rucksacks up onto her shoulders, arranged them to settle
together. I walked along with her. We did not attempt to
talk. She pointed out the mountains to me. Away beyond
the hotel the road forked north-west; if she kept on this
road she would end up aboard the ferry to the islands. But
she had known this; it was where she had been heading,
she pointed it out on her big French map of Scotland. Her
eyes bright, seeing the sun, every bit of everything.

Goodbye, she said.

I watched her walking on, bent under the weight. The
road ran straight for a long way. I sat down at the side of
it. A car passed me which when she heard she began
thumbing, doing so without either glancing at the car or
pausing in her stride. The car flashed past her. On she
walked. I waited till she was gone from my view then
lighted a cigarette. I walked down to the edge of the loch
and sat there till I finished smoking it. I strode back to the
worksite.

At the foot of the block we were working on I banged out
the signal and the hammering stopped. I crawled through
the gap and climbed the scaffolding to the platform we
were on. Chic and old Rooney sat dangling their legs over
the edge of it, smoking. Without a word I pulled on the
dungarees. As I fixed the sweatband around my neck and
forehead the old man grunted: He's saying nothing.

I know, said Chic.

Waiting for us to ask, so he is.

Aye, but look at him auld yin, he doesnt seem too pleased with himself. It must've went wrong. Eh? Did it go wrong?

Did what go wrong? I said.

That's your answer, Chic, said old Rooney; you can tell by his face. Eh, son? Am I right am I wrong?

I did not reply.

Well . . . said Chic. Did you or didnt you – that's all we're asking.

I looked at them.

Aye or no? said old Rooney.

Aye or no what? I said.

Did you or didnt you?

Did I or didnt I what?

Old Rooney shook his head. Never bother with him Chic.

I laughed.

Look at the orange bastard, cried Chic. He doesnt have to say anything.

I dont know what he makes a big secret out of it for, said old Rooney.

Chic said: You going to tell us? – aye or no! That's all we're asking.

I picked up my hammer to make sure it was properly adjusted onto the airhose and then lifted a brand new chisel out of the case. Thanks for bringing me up my gear, lads, I said. Makes a hell of a difference having a couple of good mates on a job like this.

Rooney said: You wouldnt credit it – look at him. He's not going to say a word. Last time I hand him out any tea-bags.

That goes for me too, said Chic. But how's he not telling us? Come on man – aye or no, that's all we're asking.

I inserted the chisel, began whistling.

Bastard, muttered Chic.

Ach, said the old man, who's interested anyway.

For the last time, cried Chic . . .

I had tugged the airhose and hammer across to where I had finished the last night. Slung it up across my shoulders in readiness, glanced back at them and grinned. I pulled the goggles down over my eyes and I triggered it off.

The Origin of the Axletree

Alasdair Gray

I write for anyone who knows my language. If you possess that divine knowledge do not die without teaching it to someone else. Make copies of this history, give one to anyone who can read it and read it aloud to whoever will listen. Do not be discouraged if they laugh and call you a liar. They are mostly dull herdsmen who think milk and wool more important than history. Their own history is a tangle of superstition and confused rumours. Those who lived inside the great wheel used to call them the perimeter tribes. 'Were you born outside the rim?' we would ask someone who was acting stupidly or strangely; and this question was a grave insult. The perimeter tribes lived so far from the hub that they only saw the axletree for a few months before it was completed and then only on unusually clear days. Even at sunrise its shadow never quite touched them, so now they say it was the last impiety of a mad civilization, an attack upon the heavenly gods which provoked instant punishment and defeat. But the axletree was a necessary inevitable work, soberly designed and carefully erected by statesmen, bankers, priests and many wise men whose professional names make no sense nowadays. And they completed the axletree as intended. For a moment the wheel of the civilized world was joined to the wheel of heaven. The disaster which fell a moment later was an accident nobody could have foreseen or prevented. I am the only living witness to this fact. I have been higher than anybody in the world. The hand writing these words has stroked the ice-smooth, burning-blue lucid ceiling which held up the moon.

I was born and educated at the hub of the last and greatest world empire. We had once been a republic of small farmers in a land between two lakes. Our only town in those days was a walled market with a temple in the middle where we stored the spare corn. Our land was very fertile so we developed the military virtues, first to protect our crops from neighbours, then to protect our merchants when they traded with the grain-surplus. We were also the first people to shoe horses with iron, so we soon conquered the lands round about.

Conquest is not a difficult thing – most countries have a spell of it – but an empire is only kept by careful organization, and we were good at that. We taxed the defeated people with the help of their traditional rulers, who wielded more power with our support than they could without. But the empire was mainly held by our talent for large-scale building. Captains in the army were all practical architects, and private soldiers dug ditches and built walls as steadily as they attacked the enemy under a good commander. The garrisons on foreign soil were built with stores and markets where local merchants and craftsmen could ply their trade in safety, so they became the centres of prosperous new cities. But our most important buildings were roads. All garrison towns and forts were connected by well-founded roads going straight across marsh and river by dyke and viaduct to the capital city. In two centuries these roads, radiating like spokes from a hub, were on the way to embrace the known world.

It was then we started calling our empire the great wheel. Surveyors noted that the roads tended to rise the further from the capital they got, which showed that our city was in the centre of a wide valley or hollow continent shaped like a dish. It became common for our politicians to start a speech by saying, 'This bowl of empire under this dome of heaven . . .' and end by saying, 'We have fought uphill all the way. We shall fight on till we reach the rim.' This rhetorical model of the universe became very popular, though educated people knew that the hollow continent was a large dent in the surface of a globe, a globe hanging in the centre of several hollow globes, mainly transparent, which supported the bodies of the moon, sun, planets and stars.

Then came a change of government. Our rich families had once ruled from the middle of an elected senate, but now they noticed that whoever commanded the army did not need the support of anyone else. A successful general proclaimed himself emperor. He was an efficient man with good advisers. He constructed a civil service which worked so well that trade kept flowing and the empire expanding during the reign of his son, who seems to have been a criminal lunatic who did nothing but feed his worst appetites in the most expensive ways possible. It is hard to believe that records tell the truth about this man. He was despised by the puritan aristocracy who managed the empire but loved by the common citizens. Perhaps his insane spending sprees and colossal sporting events were devised to entertain them. He also obtained remarkable tutors for his son, men of low and foreign birth but international fame. They had made a science out of history, which till then had been a branch of literature. When their pupil became third emperor he knew why his land was heading for disaster.

Many nations before ours had swelled into empires. Nearly all had collapsed while trying to defeat a country, sometimes a small one, beyond the limit of their powers. Others had enclosed the known world and then, with nothing else to conquer, had gone bad at the centre and cracked up through civil war. The emperor knew his own empire had reached a moment of ripeness. It filled the hollow continent to the rim. His roads touched the northern forests and mountains, the shores of the western sea, the baking southern desert and the wild eastern plains. The perimeter tribes lived in these places but we could not civilize them. They were nomads who could retreat forever before our army or return to their old pasture when it went away. Clearly the empire had reached its limit. The wealth of all civilization was flowing into a city with no more war to fight. The military virtues began to look foolish. The governing classes began experimenting with unhealthy pleasures. Meanwhile the emperor enlarged the circus games begun by his father in which the unemployed poor of the capital were entertained by unemployable slaves killing each other in large quantities. He also ordered from the merchants huge supplies of stone, timber and iron. The hub of the great wheel (he said) would be completely rebuilt in a grander style than ever before.

But he knew these measures could only hold the state for a short time.

A few years earlier there had appeared in our markets some pottery and cloth of such smooth, delicate and transparent textures that nobody knew how they were made. They had been brought by nomadic merchants from the eastern plains and these had obtained them, at fourth or fifth hand, from other nomads as barbarous as themselves. Enquiries produced nothing but rumour, rumour of an empire beyond so great a tract of desert, forest and mountain that it was on the far side of the globe. If rumours were true this empire was vast, rich, peaceful, and had existed without alteration for thousands of years. When the third emperor came to power his first official act had been to make ambassadors of his tutors and send them off with a strong expeditionary force to investigate the matter. Seven years passed before the embassy returned. It had shrunk to one old exhausted historian and a strange foreign servant without lids on his eyes – he shut them by making them too narrow to see through. The old man carried a letter to our emperor written in a very strange script, and he translated it.

THE EMPEROR OF THREE-RIVER KINGDOM GREETS THE EMPEROR OF THE GREAT WHEEL. I can talk to you as a friend because we are not neighbours. The distance between our lands is too great for me to fear your armies.

Your ambassadors have told me what you wish to know. Yes, my empire is very big, very rich, and also very old. This is mainly because we are a single race who talk the same language. We produce all we need inside our borders and we do not trade with foreigners. Foreign trade leads to warfare. Two nations may start trading as equals but inevitably one grows rich at the expense of the other. Then the superior nation depends on its enemy and can only maintain its profits by war or threats of war. My kingdom has survived by rejecting foreign trade. The goods which appeared in your market were smuggled out by foreigners. We will try to stop that happening again.

If your people want stability they must grow small again. Let them abandon empire and go back inside their old frontier. Let them keep an army just big enough for defence, and cultivate their own land, especially the food supply. But this is useless advice. You and I are mere emperors. We both know that a strong class of merchants and generals cannot be commanded against their will. Wealthy nations and men will embrace disaster rather than lose riches.

I regret that I cannot show you a way out of your difficulty. Perhaps the immortal gods can do that. Have you approached them? They are the last resort, but they often work for peasants, so people of our kind should not ignore them.

The emperor was startled by the last words of this intelligent and powerful man. Several countries in the empire worshipped him as a god but he was not religious. The official religion of the state had been a few simple ceremonies to help it work as smoothly as possible. An old proverb, 'Religion is the wealth of the conquered', described our view of more exotic faiths. But after we reached the rim the religions of the conquered became popular, even with our wealthy citizens. These religions had wide differences but all believed that man had descended from someone in the sky and was being punished, or taught something, by having to toil in the world below. They also believed that good people could enter a completely happy and permanent kingdom one day. Some faiths expected a leader to come from heaven, destroy all who disliked him and build a kingdom on earth for the rest. Others followed a prophet who said that after death the ghosts of their followers would enter a walled garden or city in the sky. These politically stable goals appealed to the emperor. He consulted priests in the hope that unreason would answer the question which reason could not.

He was disappointed. The priests explained that the eternal kingdom was achieved by sharing certain beliefs and ceremonies, following certain rules, and eating or avoiding certain food. People who obeyed the priests enjoyed intense feelings of satisfaction, and sometimes behaved more kindly towards those of the same faith, but even if the whole empire adopted one of these faiths the emperor did not think it would be less liable to decay and civil war. The priests mainly agreed with him. 'Only a few will enter the heavenly kingdom,' they said. The emperor wanted a kingdom for the majority. He sent agents to consult prophets and oracles in more and more outlandish places. At last he heard of a saint who lived among the perimeter tribes in a wild place which no bribe could persuade him to leave. This saint's reputation was not based on anything he taught, even by example, for he was an unpleasant person. But he had cured impotence, helped someone find a lost legacy, and shown a feeble governor how to master a difficult province. Most poeple who brought him problems were ordered rudely away, but his successes were supernaturally startling. The emperor went to see him with a troop of cavalry.

The saint was small, paunchy and bow-legged. He squatted before a crack in a rocky cliff, grinning and blinking mirthlessly, like a toad. The emperor told the soldiers to wait, went forward, knelt before the saint and talked about the problem of empire. After a silence the saint said, 'Are you strong?'

The emperor said, 'My life has been easy but my health is excellent.'

The saint felt the emperor's pulse, examined the insides of his eyelids then said gloomily, 'You are strong, yes, I can help you. But I won't enjoy it. Give me some gold.'

The emperor handed him a purse. The saint stood up and said: 'Fetch wine and oil from your men and come into my house. Tell them they won't see you till tomorrow evening. Make that perfectly clear. If they interrupt us before then you won't learn a thing. Let them pass the time making a litter to carry you in, for when you reappear you will be in a sacred condition. The expression of your face will have completely changed.'

Nobody had spoken to the emperor like that since he was a small boy and the words made him feel strangely secure. He did as he was told and then followed the saint into the crack in the rock. It led to a cave they had to stoop to enter. The saint struck a flint, lit a twisted rag in a bowl of fat, then picked up a wooden post. His dwarfish body was unusually powerful for he used the post to lever forward a great boulder till it blocked the entrance and shut out all daylight. Then he squatted with his back to the boulder and stared at the emperor across the foul-smelling lamp on the floor between them.

After a while he said, 'Tell me your last dream.'

The emperor said, 'I never dream.'

'How many tribes do you rule?'

'I rule nations, not tribes. I rule forty-three nations.'

The saint said sternly, 'Among the perimeter people a ruler who does not dream is impossible. And a ruler who dreams badly is stoned to death. Will you go away and dream well?'

The emperor stared and said, 'Is that the best you can say to me?'

'Yes.'

The emperor pointed to the boulder and said, 'Roll that thing aside. Let me out.'

'No. You have not answered my question. Will you go away and dream well?'

'I cannot command my dreams!'

'Then you cannot command yourself. And you dare to command other people?'

The saint took a cudgel from the shadows, sprang up and beat the emperor hard for a long time.

The emperor's early training had been stoical so he gasped and choked instead of screaming and yelling. Afterwards he lay against the cavern wall and gaped at the saint who had sat down to recover his breath. At last the emperor whispered, 'May I leave now?'

'But will you go away and dream well?'

'Yes. Yes, I swear I will.'

The saint groaned and said, 'You are lying. You are saying that to avoid being beaten.'

He beat the emperor again then dropped the cudgel and swigged from the wine-flask. The emperor lay with his mouth and goggling eyes wide open. He could hardly move or think but he could see that the saint was greatly distressed. The saint knelt down, placed a tender arm behind the emperor's shoulders, gently raised his head and offered wine. After swallowing some the emperor slept and was assaulted by horrible nightmares. He was among slaves killing each other in the circus to the wild cheering of the citizens. He saw his empire up on edge and bowling like a loose chariot-wheel across a stony plain. Millions of tiny people clung to the hub and to the spokes and he was among them. The wheel turned faster and faster and the tiny people fell to the rim and were whirled up again or flung to the plain where the rim rolled over them. He sobbed aloud for the only truth in the world seemed to be unending movement, unending pain. Through the pain he heard a terrible voice demand: 'Will you go away and dream well?'

He screamed: 'I *am* dreaming! I *am* dreaming!'

The voice said, 'But not well. You are dreaming the disease. Now you must dream the cure.'

And the emperor had a general impression of being beaten once more.

Later he saw the boulder had been rolled aside and that evening sunlight shone through the entrance. The saint, who had cleaned the bruises with oil, now made him drink the last of the wine. The emperor felt calm and empty. When the saint said, 'Please, please, answer my question,' the emperor shook with laughter and said, 'If you let me go I will pray *all the gods* to give me a good dream.'

The saint said, 'That is not necessary. The dream is now

travelling towards you. Only one more thing is needed to make sure it arrives.'

He beat the emperor again and the emperor did not notice, then picked the emperor up and walked from the cave and laid him on the litter prepared by the soldiers. He said to the commanding officer, 'Carry your master carefully, for he is in a very sacred condition. Write down everything he says because now his words are important. And if he recovers tell him not to apologize for what he bribed me to do. Giving men dreams is my only talent. I never have them myself.'

The emperor was carried to the hub in slow stages for he was very ill and often delirious. At the first stopping-place he dreamed of the axletree. He saw the great wheel of empire lying flat and millions of people flowing down the roads to the hub. From the hub a great smooth shaft ascended to the sky and ended in the centre of the sun. And he saw this shaft was a tower, and that everyone who had lived and died on earth was climbing up by a winding stair to the white light at the top. Then he saw this light was not the sun but a flame or flame-shaped opening in the sky, and all the people were passing through it and dissolving in the dazzling white.

For a month after his return the emperor saw nobody but doctors and the architect of the city's building pro-gramme, then he called the leaders of the empire to his bedside. His appearance shocked them. Although he had reacted against a libertine father by worrying about the work of government he had been a robust, stout, sombre, stolid man. His body was now almost starved to a skeleton, the lines of care on his face were like deep cracks in an old wooden statue, his skin, against the bank of pillows supporting him, looked livid yellow; yet he regarded the visitors with an expression of peculiar levity. His voice was so strong and hollow that he had to rest between sentences, and at these moments he sucked in his lips and bit them as if to prevent laughter. He waited until everybody was comfortably seated before speaking.

'My political researches outside the rim have damaged my kidneys and I cannot live much longer. I have decided that for a few years most of the empire's revenue will be used to build me a tomb. I invite you to form a company responsible for this building. Your time is precious, I don't expect you to give it for nothing, and, if things go as I plan, work for this company will double your present incomes. If anyone dies before the great work is completed the salary will go to his successor.'

He rested until expressions of regret, loyalty and gratitude died away then indicated some architectural drawings on the wall near the bed. He said, 'Here are the plans of the tomb. The basic shape is a steep cone with a ramp winding up. It is designed so that it can be enlarged indefinitely. I have not indicated the size of the completed work. Yourselves or posterity can decide that. My body will lie in a vault cut into the rock below the foundation. It will be a large vault, for I expect my descendants will also choose to lie there.'

He smiled at the heir to the throne then nodded kindly at the others. 'Perhaps, gentlemen, you will make the tomb so splendid that you will wish to bury yourselves and your families in chambers adjacent to mine. Indeed, I would like even quite humble people who help the great effort to end under it, although their graves will naturally be narrower and less well furnished than ours. But you will decide these things. As to the site of the structure, it will be in the exact centre of the city, the exact centre of the empire. Has the high priest of war and thunder anything to say?'

The head of the state religion shrugged uneasily and said, 'Sir, everyone knows that spot is the most sacred in the empire. My temple stands there. It was built by the hero who founded our nation. Will you knock it down?'

The emperor said, 'I will rebuild it on a grander scale than ever before. The space above the burial chambers will be a pantheon to all the gods of our heaven and empire, for a great building must serve the living as well as the dead or nobody will take it seriously for long. And my tomb will have room for more than a temple, even though that temple is the biggest in the world. Look again at the plans. The temple is the circular *core* of the building. Vast stone piers radiate from it, piers spanned by arching vaults and pierced by arched doors. The spaces between the piers can be made wide enough to hold markets, factories and assembly rooms. These spaces are linked by curving avenues ascending at a slope gradual enough to race horses up. As you know, when I came to the throne I swore to rebuild our city on a grander scale than ever before. And what is a city but a great house shared by a community? The wealthy will have mansions in it, the poor can rent apartments. Parks and gardens will be planted along the outer terraces. And you, the building committee, will have your offices in the summit. As this rises higher the whole administration of the empire will move in beneath you . . . But a dying man should not look so far ahead. What do our businessmen say? Can they supply the materials to build on an increasingly large scale for generations to come? Can they provide food for a steadily enlarging labour force? I ask the heads of the corn and stock exchanges to give an opinion. Don't consider the matter as salaried members of the building company, but as managers of the empire's trade.'

* * *

Towards the end of the emperor's speech the faces of the leading businessmen had acquired a dreamy, speculative look, but the head of the stock exchange roused himself and said, 'We can tackle that, certainly, if the government pay us to do so.'

Everyone looked at the civil service chief who was also the imperial accountant. He said slowly, 'Ever since our armies reached the rim our provinces have been complaining about the heavy taxation. We could once justify that by attacking enemies outside the borders. We have no enemies now, but if we allow the provinces to grow rich they will break away from us. Yes, we can certainly finance this structure. And there will be no shortage of labour. We are already paying huge doles to the unemployed, merely to stop them revolting against us.'

The commander of the armed forces said, 'Will expenditure on this building require a reduction of the armed forces?'

The imperial accountant said, 'Oh no! The army may even have to be enlarged, to keep the taxes coming in.'

'Then I like the idea. The emperor has called the structure a great house. I call it a castle. At present the city has overflowed the old fortifications, our hub is a sprawling, indefensible mess. A high walled city will not only be easier to defend, it could be easier to police. Let the great doors between the different levels of the structure have heavy portcullises in them. Then with very little effort we can imprison and starve any part of the population which gets out of hand.'

'But the outer walls must be faced with shining marble!' cried the head of the arts council. 'If it looks beautiful from a distance I am sure foreign provinces will gladly let us continue taking their food, materials and men at the old cheap rate. Everyone wants to admire something wonderful, support something excellent, be part of something splendid which will not fail or die. Are you alright, sir?'

The emperor was shuddering with what seemed silent laughter but his teeth rattled and his brows sweated so it was probably fever. When he recovered he apologized and said, 'Now I will tell you a dream I had.'

He told them the dream of the axletree.

'Sir!' said the high priest in an inspired voice. 'You have given the empire a new way to grow! You have offered a solution to the political problem of the age, and mentioned the dream which gave the idea as an afterthought. But all dreams are sacred, and the dreams of a ruler are most sacred of all. Perhaps the heavenly gods are growing lonely. Perhaps mankind is becoming fit to join them. Let us tell the world this dream. You may be the prophet who will lead us all to the golden garden in the sky.'

'I like that idea,' said the emperor languidly. 'And, certainly, let people know the dream occurred. But don't explain it, at this stage. You would antagonize religions whose prophet has already arrived. When the temple part of the building is completed dedicate it to the gods and their true prophet, but avoid mentioning names. Keep the official religion a kind of *cavity* which other religions can hope to fill if they grow big enough. But you mentioned gold. In spite of his mad spending my father left a fortune which I have been able to increase. I want it all converted into gold and placed beside my body in the vault. Let people know that the building company can use it in emergencies. But never do so. The fact that it exists and you own it will give the company more power over men than mere spending could give. Lend on the security of this gold, borrow on the security of this gold, if creditors press you hard *cheat* upon the security of this gold, but never, never touch it.'

* * *

The emperor closed his eyes and seemed to doze. The politicians whispered to each other. Suddenly he cried out in a great voice: 'Do not call it a tower! Towers are notorious for falling down. Tell the fools you are building a connection between two absolutely dependable things. Call it an axletree.'

Then he giggled faintly and said, 'I suppose one day the world will be governed by people whose feet have never touched the ground. I wonder what will happen if there is a sky, and they reach it . . . I wonder what the child will look like.'

He died a few hours later.

And there was a sky, and in two thousand years we reached it. And though hardly anybody understands my language, everybody knows what happened after that.

A Day by the Sea

Scoular Anderson

The girl had rung the bell but now stood silent on the step before the open door. For a moment she glanced back over her shoulder as if appealing for a cue from the world in general, then she turned to where Lilian stood with the door ajar at what she thought was a respectable distance in the circumstances. How they struggled, these women, not only to find words that would open lines of communication but also to extricate themselves from a situation they couldn't handle. The little glass porch in which they stood was filling up with water. They were out of their depths and they were drowning.

'A'm waitin' for ma sister,' said the girl at last, but that was all she was going to offer. Lilian reflected that she, too, was waiting for her sister but this common experience brought them no closer together and the safety of dry land hovered far in the distance. The angular panes of glass around them stabbed and picked at their faces with mauve and sepia lights.

'My sister is away for the day,' Lilian decided to explain as her fingers lightly knotted themselves round her floral brooch of cut coral. 'She is usually in charge.'

That was a long-accepted fact and she threw out the sentence with conviction though the words carried a ballast of lead.

Lilian had never been left alone in the house for at least twenty years. Now she was alone and in charge as Bel had gone out of town to consult a lawyer.

'I will manage,' Lilian had said as she arranged the clamminess of damp dish-towels on the rails beside the kitchen sink. Bel was furiously checking the contents of her handbag and her silence reeked heavily of doubt.

'You are not used to it. You are not used to managing, are you?' The way Bel addressed the question to the small change in her purse rather than her sister implied that she was unarguably right and didn't require an answer.

Now there was an unforeseen hazard: a stranger at the door. Lilian felt what little experience she had of life, shredding like pulled gauze beneath her feet.

Her elder sister, who ploughed through life as a demolition expert's metal ball would plough through a gable end, had felt it necessary to protect Lilian from the ravages of the outer world. Lilian was tender. That was Bel's description. 'The world is full of such uglinesses!' was one of her favourite sayings. 'And tender flowers must be protected.' Somewhere in the middle of that belief lay true affection perhaps. It was an area in which Lilian had long since ceased to explore. Their long spinsterhood spent together had sealed off certain avenues. On the whole, Bel treated her as a child: with condescension, primly, criticizing her every move. The only thing about Lilian over which she would occasionally enthuse was her cooking, but even then it was as if she was praising some piece of precision-made machinery, allotted a certain task in life and in which failure should be regarded as unthinkable. Lilian therefore lived out her days in her kitchen, happily enough, as she had done in every boarding-house they had run together.

The girl was still silent on the doorstep. The sea beyond her head changed colour and changed again as the effect of sunlight between showers and strong gusts of wind laid out swathes of greys on the water.

Lilian had decided at this point to make a dash for dry land. Perhaps it was her impulsive nature that Bel had tried to lock away. 'On the spur of the moment' was a phrase that Lilian used often, wielding it like a rusty claymore in some frantic defence of her actions.

'I made this on the spur of the moment . . . I saw the recipe . . .' And her words would die away, just as her sword, so unmanageably large, would whirl her off balance as it crashed and shattered against her sister's insurmountable shell, from behind which, eyes stared down stonily on some confection on the kitchen table, obviously too adventurously decadent to set before guests at a seaside boarding-house.

Spurs of moments were anathemas to Bel, conjuring up spiky disaster.

'You take after Father,' she would snap. 'Look where impulsive action got him.'

'He was a naval officer,' said Lilian. 'I would have thought that drowning was an occupational hazard.'

'Heroic drowning, yes,' said Bel tartly. 'But to decide on an impulse to shift course so that he could identify a flotilla of strange duck then collide with the outer wall of a harbour can be nothing but embarrassing. And in broad daylight,' she added to adjust the insult sufficiently.

Lilian spared a brief thought for twisted iron and gurgling foam.

It could have been jealousy that made Bel puncture Lilian with shortcomings. While Lilian hummed around her kitchen, Bel would move through the upper rooms, among furniture and guests, like an invigilator at a school examination, eys daring a particle of cigarette ash to fall, a spot of dust to settle. Daily business was mentally listed and the list strictly adhered to. There was no room for deviation. There would be no surprises. Lilian's little improvisations must have seemed, at times, either wildly erratic misdemeanours, or else something she longed to share. Again and again, memories of her father would surface: the vulgar little man, arriving home from the other side of the globe, arms loaded with knick-knacks and bottles, blustering in on a cloud of tobacco smoke. Then, not half-an-hour later, the guests: passengers on his ship that he had taken a fancy to and invited to stay for a few days. The whole messy homecoming: glasses of sherry and rum; souvenirs unparcelled, crooned over with temporary enthusiasm, shortly to be forgotten; piles of exotic wrapping-paper on the floor; strange men whose eyes roved on the flesh of the captain's daughters; mysterious women in the bathroom, their scents and powders thick upon the tiles; the preparation of endless meals – afternoon teas sandwiched between long lunches and port-coloured suppers.

The fact that running a boarding-house had perhaps evolved from her early apprenticeship in dealing with her father's guests had never entered Bel's mind. Or maybe it had tried but had been firmly repulsed. At least, no longer did guests turn up quite so suddenly and Bel was in complete control as far as the choice of guest was concerned. She would never have let a strange girl cross the threshold. Lilian's impulse was to open the door wider, inviting entry.

'Your sister . . .?' she asked vaguely, politeness suffocating her curiosity.

'She told me to wait for her,' said the girl.

'Here?'

'Aye.'

This seemed a perfectly reasonable arrangement. Lilian was willing to trust the initiative of others.

'Would you like to come in and sit down then?' she asked.

The girl didn't answer but came up the steps. As they disappeared inside, the hydrangeas that swarmed down either side of the path raised the skulls of last year's unpruned flowers in judgement.

Lilian made a wide circuit round the girl to open the glass door of the lounge and lead the way in. Around the pink coral brooch on the collar of her blouse, her fingers fluttered, a fleshy butterfly on a most impotent flower.

The girl chose the nearest chair and sat down, far enough away from the plumped cushion as to leave it unsullied. Lilian sat down opposite her, she couldn't think why. The girl looked at her with hostility while she could only stare. On the whole, her life was peopled with jolly grocers and helpful postmen. The girl was a new species she had not encountered and therefore was to be investigated. The little lounge, bland enough to assume any role thrust upon it, for a moment became a zoo and the girl a mélange of its inmates.

Lilian let sensations swell. As she stared, she felt the tingling fear she reserved for reptiles; she sensed the safely distant friendship she summoned up for simians. There were, however, a few doubts – about things like Maribu storks: how lice-ridden were these feathers? – that beak of an unhealthy tattiness! The girl's face was not unlike a beak; thin, reddish skin pulled tautly over fragile but spiky bones. Her hair and fashionable clothes had been dampened by rain. Lilian felt that if she picked at a piece of skin, she would be able to unpeel everything and find something infinitely more likeable inside.

'Would you like a cup of tea?' she asked, realizing that the girl was no longer a menagerie.

'Aye, OK,' said the girl, shrugging.

Lilian whirled off the sofa, now beginning to desire freedom. As she went out into the hall, the doubts, at last, began to filter through. Was the girl to be trusted? Would she stuff the precious faience inkwell into her pocket? She turned quickly and came back. The girl's concrete pose filled her with shame.

'Won't be a moment,' she croaked, and disappeared again.

As Lilian lifted the tea-caddy from the shelf her mind swerved to avoid something unpleasant. The girl was now standing at the kitchen door – her kitchen door. She felt assaulted somehow. The angle at which the girl was leaning against the door frame made the kitchen seem even more prim and tidy than usual. The rectangles of Fablon and Formica lay with garish tautness in all directions.

'Do you mind broken orange pekoe? We usually keep the assam for evening,' Lilian found herself saying. Then she coloured slightly with embarrassment. The girl's stone-faced incomprehension made her words slubber about the room like a demented balloon. She was horrified how this stranger was bringing out the worst in her. She felt like a rouged puppet, capering, as if trying to compensate for the lack of expression on the girl's face.

She began to fluster. Cups didn't match saucers on the tray. The milk slopped in the sugar bowl. When the hideous tea-making ceremony was over, Lilian picked up the tray and made for the door but was checked by the sight of the girl settled at the kitchen table, lighting up a cigarette. Any sign of life was to be encouraged, she thought. She came back quickly to lay the tray on the table and sit down.

'Now,' she said and paused with her hands clasped. 'Milk?'

'Aye.'

'Very cold. Rawish weather,' said Lilian as she arranged cups.

'Are you warm enough in those clothes?' she continued, not so much with genuine concern but hoping to coax some biological information from an alien species.

'Sugar?'

'Aye.'

'Two?'

'Aye. That'll do.'

Lilian pushed the cup towards the girl.

'From Glasgow are you?' she asked.

'Aye. Just down for the day,' said the girl.

'How nice. A day by the sea – but unfortunately so cold.'

When Lilian had poured her own tea, they sipped in silence. For a moment, the presence of the girl let Lilian flutter, pullet-like, on a flight of fancy. The gift of the knife was in her hands. She played through her mind what would happen if Bel at that moment returned. Lilian would lift her eyes with the air of a seasoned society hostess: 'This is . . . [here, she realized she didn't even know the girl's name] . . . she just popped in as she was waiting for her sister . . .' Incongruities suddenly bunched up like fleshy weeds: this girl, the strangest of silent guests, sitting in the middle of the kitchen; the fact that Lilian should have a guest at all; the sister that would appear, presently. It occurred to Lilian that she might now safely ask about the sister, but the girl spoke first.

'It's a big kitchen.'

'It is,' said Lilian and sipped. 'A big kitchen.'

The girl was robbing her of conversation. She felt she was being chipped, like a block of wood. She was being sculpted, identifying her new shape from the formless lump she seemed to remember being. She was all edged, new and sharp.

'Have you been here before?' Lilian tried again.

'Nuh,' said the girl. Then as if to ward off any more questions, she proffered: 'Ma sister has been here hundreds of times. But a havney.'

'The beach is quite pleasant,' said Lilian. 'Rocky, but quite pleasant and the prom is nice to walk along.'

How rat-like the girl had become, and without a handbag, Lilian noticed. The girl stubbed out her cigarette in the saucer. For a second, Lilian saw a child's face and wanted to touch it.

'You're not very old,' she said.

'Old enough,' said the girl. 'It's none of your business, anyway.'

Lilian was bewildered and during this hiatus in the charade, voices were heard drifting in from the distance, dropping down softly from the open top of the kitchen window. There was the sound of scuffed gravel.

'Someone's coming up the path,' said Lilian, her ear well-tuned to the sounds around the house.

'It'll be ma sister,' said the girl with hope rather than conviction.

'It was a man's voice I heard,' said Lilian firmly as she rose from the table, scraping the folds of her mouth with a handkerchief produced from a sleeve. The girl was rising from the table too.

'Finish your tea,' said Lilian, motherly now.

The bell writhed briefly in the dimness of hall and passageway as Lilian moved towards the front door. She opened it wide and in came the sea: a network of currents today; an uncertain sequence of drift and flow. Just as Lilian had begun to feel the safety of dry land beneath her feet, the waters came to close about her once more.

'It's ma sister,' said the girl from behind Lilian's left shoulder. Lilian followed the words to where they pointed.

The extra two men beside the sister conjured up conspiracy. Lilian composed her face but the sister was already advancing through the glass porch.

Followed by her aides, she moved into the hall as if expecting the familiar yet not finding it. She glanced around then looked at Lilian to confirm the match. She became briefly interested in the inlaid wooden tea-box on the hall table, lifting the lid, but disappointed in the secrecy of the empty green felt interior, let the lid snap shut. Her jaws at last, for a moment, ceased to chew.

'You werney here last time,' she said and stood, awaiting results.

Lilian was forcibly dragged back from nearby mental alleys, down which she was attempting to escape.

'No, only two seasons,' she said. 'We've only had this establishment two seasons.'

'It was Mrs Mackellar's place last time,' said the sister as if accusing. 'You know, her place,' she added with a heaviness which carried the equivalent value of a wink.

Lilian's naïvety carried her above such gross subtleties. She sensed that danger was near, however; its presence but not its form was becoming clear. She was hating this woman's icy eyes, made even more colourless by the surrounds of blue and black eye paint. The sister took another twirl round the hallway as she made a decision. She returned to stand before Lilian.

'We want a couple of rooms,' she said, more of a dare than a request.

The outside world came battering into the genteel shadows of the hall. Lilian's fingers ripped at the pink coral. She now became exceedingly aware of the two young men, standing with unsure arrogance, thumbs tucked into the pockets of their jeans. They were Americans, from the Base. Even Lilian knew that.

The apparent horror of the situation made her reckless. To her surprise, from a solid wooden throat, she found herself aiming a dart over the sister's head.

'From the ship, are you?' she asked the men.

Their clothes rustled self-consciously as they found themselves the centre of attention.

'My father was a sea-captain,' Lilian almost shrieked, trying to delay the inevitable. 'But he was drowned when he collided with a mole.'

She was unaware of her capering words while the others grappled with unwieldy images.

'What about the rooms?' said the sister with almost a snap.

'Rooms? Oh, rooms!' said Lilian.

Her innocence still buoyed her up. It still shone around, bright enough to dazzle her enemies. Her enemies would be dazzled, she decided. Oh, how the knife-blade shone. She fumbled with the reservations book on the hall table. She knew perfectly well that the place was completely empty being so early in the season but she felt a formality would be comforting.

'Rooms 4 and 5,' she said. 'I'll take you up.'

'We'll manage,' said the sister who already had her foot on the bottom step. They ascended quickly.

'We'll pay later,' said the sister from the top landing.

The blatant mention of money was the final vulgarity Lilian could hardly handle. Why, even ordinary guests were silently handed the bill, face down on a discreet plate.

Part of Lilian's mind became a wash-cloth thrown over something unpleasant to mop up and conceal, but the unpleasantness came through slowly, forming a stain. She heard the shutting of mystery-laden bedroom doors and an awful silence lay down like a huge mattress on the landing and the stair.

Lilian moved off into her kitchen and busied herself in tasks. When the kitchen was comfortably filled with the smell of warm ironing she could detach herself from the tainted house around her. She could recall days by the sea. She could let the breaking waves and the crabwise slither of water across flat sand and the tumbling wind free her and absolve her. When the pit of her stomach had ceased to writhe like hot magma and the rods of glass inside her head had ceased to press, her purgatory was complete. She opened the kitchen door and walked up the passageway and into the hall.

The two women had come downstairs and were now sitting on the garden seat in front of the glass porch. The men were still upstairs, Lilian could imagine at last, lying among the wild sheets, smoking.

The young girl twisted round and knelt, her knees on the seat, her arms folded on the seat's back.

'Gerry!' her voice sounded shrill against the bedroom windows. 'Gerry, come and take our photos!'

Lilian heard a murmur from above but as yet, no movement.

'Gerry!' the girl persisted. 'Go on, Gerry. Come and take our photos.'

At last Lilian heard the movement of feet on the floor and a window opening. The girl and her sister simpered and posed below the invisible camera, lolling on the seat. Lilian could imagine these terrible snapshots already being noted down as evidence, because, from the taxi at the gate, Bel was emerging like a Greek myth: a complex of terrible darkness, accusation, grudge, wrath, retribution, tweed folds and glinting pearls. Even before she had closed the gate she had come to grips with the situation. Her feet smashed horribly on the gravel as she came up the pathway. Never had the early tulips looked so subservient. As she approached the house her face became blotched, like a peeled orange. Between the drifts of pithy powder, acid spurted.

Only briefly, as the front door swung open, did Lilian remember slaters, scrabbling vulnerably on their backs when the stone above them is overturned. She remained standing there, in the softness of the hallway where she had been for some time. Then, when Bel had passed her and the leather of handbag and gloves was clicking furiously on the table behind her, she ventured to speak.

'There was a mistake,' she said, almost brightly.

Bel coughed or choked or had difficulty with her teeth.

'I might have known,' she managed to squeeze out at last between ridged lips. 'I go away for a matter of hours and you succeed in turning the house into . . .' The sentence never had the intention of being complete.

Bel contorted grotesquely with her hatpins while Lilian continued to stand, observing the subtleties of sea beyond the glowing porch.

Not until the guests had been ushered, or rather, flushed out and Bel was ripping sheets and blankets from beds and opening wide certain windows did Lilian return to her kitchen, to be embraced by its familiar air, and prepare for tea.

Taken into Care

Eric Woolston

'Get out, will you. Go on. I'll thrash you if you're late for
school.'

It was the only thing the woman had said to her
daughter since shaking her awake. Swallowing the last of
her lumpy porridge and the lard-smeared crust, Elsie set
out on her two-mile walk. Her sisters were older and went
to the other school, except the eldest, Elaine, who stayed
at home with her baby; it had no known father. The long
trek was a bleak start to the ten-year-old's day, which
would end as bleakly with her mother's bitterness at
seeing her return that evening.

On the road it was better. When the sun shone the fells
looked green and bright; and there were roadside flowers.
Alone was better than with Mother.

She didn't hear the motor cycle until the roaring died
down. Then she looked up and saw that it had stopped. A
man was sitting astride the still-throbbing engine.

'Are you goin' to schoo'?' He spoke grotesquely, as if
he had no roof to his mouth.

She nodded. His trousers were dirty down the fly, like
Dad's had been before he cleared off. The shirt neck
was open. Dirty, too. You could see black, curly hair
inside.

'Come f'r a ri'? See my house?' He pointed to the
sidecar. She could get in there.

He didn't look nasty, or nice either. She didn't feel

frightened or excited. School or his house, she didn't care. She found herself climbing in.

They didn't speak during the ride. It wasn't long and there was nothing to say. She liked feeling the wind in her face and the way the fells seemed higher because she was sitting low in the sidecar. She liked sitting next to someone – someone who had *asked* her to. That was something new.

He turned into a side-lane and then into a field. The building must be his house. Downstairs it looked like a barn, with a big door standing open and high-piled bales of hay inside. Up some steps on the first floor there was a balcony and opening on to it a door and some windows.

'Do you live upstairs?'

It was her first question for months. She scarcely spoke a word at home and never asked questions at school. It was all too boring. Twice recently the teacher had come and talked to her individually, frowning, wanting to know things. Not just about lessons; about home, too. She didn't like the teacher talking to her, trying to find out about her; you couldn't be close to a teacher. She looked at the man expressionlessly. Perhaps he would be different.

He didn't say anything but led her through the big door into the barn. Inside, he took her hand.

It was mainly hay there. But far back in the shadows there was a loft overhanging like the gallery of a cinema and below it there lay a wide mattress and on it bedclothes and a pillow. On a couple of boxes nearby lay washing and shaving tackle and a man's vest.

'Is it where you live?'

'Yes.'

With a look of respect she tilted her gaze up at him and then after a moment's thought slowly set her school satchel down beside the boxes. Somehow, it was an action which sealed their friendship.

He showed her round the barn, the farmyard and for several hours the neighbouring fields, drenched with sun. They scarcely spoke at all. Once she wondered about school, but only vaguely. Going back would mean getting a note to explain her absence and her mother couldn't write. It didn't matter.

They met nobody all day. Only once in the barn she heard him talking to a woman upstairs in the house. She seemed to be ranting at him. When he came down he pulled a sour face and shrugged.

'Mother,' he said, explaining.

In the evening he brought her, from upstairs, bread and ham and apples and made tea on an oilstove. In the dusk they munched happily, watching the red westerly glow streaked with purple clouds.

Elsie said, 'Are you taking me back now?'

He indicated the mattress. 'Stay here.'

She looked at it. It seemed all right.

'Yes.'

After they finished their tea he took her to a tap at the back of the barn and gave her some soap. He didn't shout at her like her mother. No other kids, either. No Elaine. She missed that, not having Elaine and the baby. Tentatively she washed her hands and face in the trickling water. Then she dried herself and he led her back to the barn.

'What's your name?' she said.

'Paul.'

He pointed to one side of the mattress. 'You slee' there.'

He took the soap and towel and went out for his own wash. Elsie hesitated for several minutes. It was different

from home, not a proper house. But she didn't mind it. It
was even rather nice. A bit adventurous. She took off her
dress, shoes and socks and keeping her underclothes on slid
into bed on the side he had pointed to. She kept very near
the edge so as not to bump into him. By the time he came
back she was fast asleep.

When she awoke there were patches of sunshine on the
floor of the barn. Paul was already dressed and making tea.
While it was brewing he went upstairs and brought down
bread and some jam. This time she heard the woman's
scoldings distinctly.

'No need to lie to me. I know you've got a woman there.
As if I haven't trouble enough. You do nothing, just like
your father was. Then you come begging food from me.'

But he got the food just the same.

'What do you do?' Elsie asked.

'Pick thin's up. Clothes. Thin's.' Then he added. 'You
c'n come.'

But he didn't seem to mean now. After breakfast Elsie
had scarcely had time to slip on her dress while he was not
looking when suddenly he stood stock-still, as if listening to
something. Then, quickly lifting her up by the armpits, he
carried her to his motorbike and thrust her into the sidecar,
covering her instantly with the waterproof cover.

She heard a man come round to the door of the barn, two
men, talking.

'No,' Paul said, 'no.'

'A little girl . . . ten years old . . . Since yesterday
morning.'

Elsie smiled. It was *her*. This was exciting, being
searched for. She thrilled silently inside herself. Soon the
men went and when Paul let her out he grinned and winked
at her broadly. What *fun*!

They didn't leave the farm that day and Paul again begged meals from his mother. He brought Elsie an extra box for her things and a separate towel and washed her socks, laying them out to dry in the hay. In the evening they played dominoes.

That night she was not asleep when he returned from washing. She averted her eyes as he stripped; but when, later, he reached for her in the dark she cuddled up, indifferently at first but by morning with warmth and gratitude. Waking once in the night she found his hand lying between her legs. But it wasn't uncomfortable for her and so, not wanting to wake him, she left it there.

Summer changed to autumn without Elsie ever questioning her new life or thinking much of home. In her leisure she enjoyed walking in the copper-turning woods or racing twigs down the stream with Paul. She began to laugh at things. One day the two of them narrowly escaped a search-party beating the fields for someone. But it was the only time: after that there were no more searches.

She often accompanied Paul in the sidecar when he went out 'picking things up'. He scavenged mainly from dustbins and would get up early on the morning when the bins were put out so as to be there before the dustmen. Sometimes he visited hotel dustbins at Leadenscar, sometimes factory refuse-heaps. From his searches he brought home odd pieces of furniture, old clothes, half worn-out shoes, rusting metal fittings and a vast variety of other oddments from old spectacles to beaten-up electric fires and bent table-knives. Some things he kept for himself or his mother; others he sold in dingy little shops in Lidby. On the money he got they could manage.

Elsie, useless at first, slowly learnt to judge what might sell and what price it might fetch. He rewarded her

progress by showing a pleasure which silently strength-
ened the bond between them. He did what he could to
make her comfortable, made coffee in the morning because she preferred it to tea, heated her washing water,
bought her chocolate and a new jumper.

'Have you lived here always?' she asked.

'Except the Army. Nationa' Service.'

'Have you had jobs? Proper jobs?'

'On'y this. Pickin' thin's up. Like Dad.' Then, hopelessly, he added, 'It's no goo', pickin' thin's up. I'm no
goo'.'

When, one day, his mother saw Elsie for the first time
she turned white, as if with anger, but grimly refused to
say anything. She still gave them milk and food from time
to time.

Once, Paul brought her a letter and being himself
unable to read asked her to read it to him.

'Swetenham's Marriage Bureau,' it said.

> Dear Sir,
>   Further to ours of the 4th inst., we write to remind
> you of the sum of £100 still owing to us on account of
> your registration here and request immediate pay-
> ment.

'You owe them it. £100.' The size of the debt staggered
her.

He made a noise of assent, shrugged and crumpling the
letter up threw it on the floor. That night in bed she asked,
'Do you want to get married?'

He looked at her with a strange, sad longing and
nodded.

'No women, me. Never. Be'er ge' married.' Then, 'An'
you?'

'I want a baby, like Elaine.'

He nodded and they drew closer together. During the night she was puzzled at how hard his body, down in the groin, pressed against her, but he did nothing, then or any other night, only held her with a slow, heartbroken tenderness.

As the months passed Elsie sensed that her world was changing. This life here was better, safer. She felt sure of Paul, he would always be there, he wouldn't leave her. And she was free to come and go, to do as she pleased. Even the work she enjoyed, finding things, getting money. It had kindled a spark of interest in the outside world. She began to admire things they collected, an old crocheted shawl, a glass necklace, a pair of pewter candlesticks. Once or twice she tried to communicate her love of things to Paul, but he only grunted indifferently.

It was her awakening sense of wonder and the urge to explore things that bred in her a fateful habit. Returning from scavenging late one November afternoon, they stopped at a nearby village; and while Paul went to buy some food Elsie let her gaze be drawn into the brightly lit windows of the shops. She was enthralled. The brilliance, the glossy pictures, the colours; the glamour of a world of wealth, all were a new, heady magic to her. From that moment on, her greatest delight was on any pretext to stand endlessly peering into those windows. One evening when Paul happened to be away she set out, of her own accord, to walk to the village, bent on window-gazing. It was her first journey of any length on foot, unconcealed by the hood of the sidecar. On the way the driver of a passing car recognized her from pictures he had seen in the press and took her, all unresisting, to the nearest police station.

The law moved quickly. Paul was brought to trial for abduction, though charges of assault and carnal knowledge were quickly dropped and the prosecuting counsel's account of him as a sordid exploiter rang strangely false in court. Expert witnesses on his mental state hedged with frosty uneasiness. Elsie and Paul were allowed to meet briefly in court. There they stood, mute and estranged, already divided by the lonely world to which they had been returned, their brief season of devotion and tenderness almost forgotten. But justice was satisfied. Paul, for his offences, was sentenced to four years of imprisonment while for Elsie, on account of hers, was reserved the destiny of being, in the clipped judicial phrase, 'taken into care'.

A Time to Dance

Bernard MacLaverty

Nelson, with a patch over one eye, stood looking idly into Mothercare's window. The sun was bright behind him and made a mirror out of the glass. He looked at his patch with distaste and felt it with his finger. The elastoplast was rough and dry and he disliked the feel of it. Bracing himself for the pain, he ripped it off and let a yell out of him. A woman looked down at him curiously to see why he had made the noise but by that time he had the patch in his pocket. He knew without looking that some of his eyebrow would be on it.

He had spent most of the morning in the Gardens avoiding distant uniforms but now that it was coming up to lunchtime he braved it on to the street. He had kept his patch on longer than usual because his mother had told him the night before that if he didn't wear it he would go 'stark, staring blind'.

Nelson was worried because he knew what it was like to be blind. The doctor at the eye clinic had given him a box of patches that would last for most of his lifetime. Opticludes. One day Nelson had worn two and tried to get to the end of the street and back. It was a terrible feeling. He had to hold his head back in case it bumped into anything and keep waving his hands in front of him backwards and forwards like windscreen wipers. He kept tramping on tin cans and heard them trundle emptily away. Broken glass crackled under his feet and he could not figure out how close to the wall he was. Several times he heard footsteps approaching, slowing down as if they were going to attack him in his helplessness, then walking away. One of the footsteps even laughed. Then he heard a voice he knew only too well.

'Jesus, Nelson, what are you up to this time?' It was his mother. She led him back to the house with her voice blaring in his ear.

She was always shouting. Last night, for instance, she had started into him for watching TV from the side. She had dragged him round to the chair in front of it.

'That's the way the manufacturers make the sets. They put the picture on the front. But oh no, that's not good enough for our Nelson. He has to watch it from the side. Squint, my arse, you'll just go blind – stark, staring blind.'

Nelson then had turned his head and watched it from the front. She had never mentioned the blindness before. Up until now all she had said was 'If you don't wear them patches that eye of yours will turn in till it's looking at your brains. God knows, not that it'll have much to look at.'

His mother was Irish. That was why she had a name like Skelly. That was why she talked funny. But she was proud of the way she talked and nothing angered her more than to hear Nelson saying 'Ah ken' and 'What like is it?' She kept telling him that someday they were going back when she had enough ha'pence scraped together. 'Until then I'll not let them make a Scotchman out of you.' But Nelson talked the way he talked.

His mother had called him Nelson because she said she thought that his father had been a seafaring man. The day the boy was born she had read an article in the *Reader's Digest* about Nelson Rockefeller, one of the richest men in the world. It seemed only right to give the boy a good start. She thought it also had the advantage that it couldn't be shortened, but she was wrong. Most of the boys in the scheme called him Nelly Skelly.

He wondered if he should sneak back to school for dinner then skive off again in the afternoon. They had good dinners at school – like a hotel, with choices. Chips and magic things like rhubarb crumble. There was one big dinner-woman who gave him extra every time she saw him. She told him he needed fattening. The only drawback to the whole system was that he was on free dinners. Other people in his class were given their dinner money and it was up to them whether they went without a dinner and bought Coke and sweets and stuff with the money. It was a choice Nelson didn't have, so he had to invent other things to get the money out of his mother. In Lent there was the Black Babies; library fines were worth the odd 10p although, as yet, he had not taken a book from the school library – and anyway they didn't have to pay fines even if they were late; the Home Economics Department asked them to bring in money to buy their ingredients and Nelson would always add 20p to it.

'What the hell are they teaching you to cook – sides of beef?' his mother would yell. Outdoor pursuits required extra money. But even though they had ended after the second term Nelson went on asking for the 50p on a Friday – 'to go horse-riding'. His mother would never part with money without a speech of some sort.

'Horse riding? Horse riding! Jesus, I don't know what sort of a school I've sent you to. Is Princess Anne in your class or something? Holy God, horse riding.'

Outdoor pursuits was mostly walking round museums on wet days and, when it was dry, the occasional trip to Portobello beach to write on a flapping piece of foolscap the signs of pollution you could see. Nelson felt that the best outdoor pursuit of the lot was what he was doing now. Skiving. At least that way, you could do what you liked.

He groped into his pocket for the change out of his 50p and went into a shop. He bought a giant thing of bubble-gum and crammed it into his mouth. It was hard and dry at first and he couldn't answer the woman when she spoke to him.

'Whaaungh?'

'Pick the paper off the floor, son! Use the basket.'

He picked the paper up and screwed it into a ball. He aimed to miss the basket, just to spite her, but it went in. By the time he reached the bottom of the street the gum was chewy. He thrust his tongue into the middle of it and blew. A small disappointing bubble burst with a plip. It was not until the far end of Princes Street that he managed to blow big ones, pink and wobbling, that he could see at the end of his nose which burst well and had to be gathered in shreds from his chin.

Then suddenly the crowds of shoppers parted and he saw his mother. In the same instant she saw him. She was on him before he could even think of running. She grabbed him by the fur of his parka jacket and began screaming into his face.

'In the name of God Nelson what are you doing here? Why aren't you at school?' She began shaking him. 'Do you realize what this means? They'll put me in bloody jail. It'll be bloody Saughton for me, and no mistake.' She had her teeth gritted together and her mouth was slanting in her face. Then Nelson started to shout.

'Help! Help!' he yelled.

A woman with an enormous chest like a pigeon stopped. 'What's happening?' she said.

Nelson's mother turned on her. 'It's none of your bloody business.'

'I'm being kidnapped,' yelled Nelson.

'Young woman. Young woman . . .' said the lady with the large chest trying to tap Nelson's mother on the shoulder with her umbrella, but Mrs Skelly turned with such a snarl that the woman edged away hesitatingly and looked over her shoulder and tut-tutted just loudly enough for the passing crowd to hear her.

'Help! I'm being kidnapped,' screamed Nelson, but everybody walked past looking the other way. His mother squatted down in front of him, still holding on to his jacket. She lowered her voice and tried to make it sound reasonable.

'Look Nelson, love. Listen. If you're skiving school do you realize what'll happen to me? In Primary the Children's Panel threatened to send me to court. You're only at that Secondary and already that Sub-Attendance Committee thing wanted to fine me. Jesus if you're caught again . . .'

Nelson stopped struggling. The change in her tone had quietened him down. She straightened up and looked wildly about her, wondering what to do.

'You've got to go straight back to school, do you hear me?'

'Yes.'

'Promise me you'll go.' The boy looked down at the ground. 'Promise?' The boy made no answer.

'I'll kill you if you don't go back. I'd take you myself only I've my work to go to. I'm late as it is.'

Again she looked around as if she would see someone who would suddenly help her. Still she held on to his jacket. She was biting her lip.

'O God, Nelson.'

The boy blew a flesh-pink bubble and snapped it between his teeth. She shook him.

'That bloody bubble gum.'

There was a loud explosion as the one o'clock gun went off. They both leapt.

'O Jesus, that gun puts the heart sideways in me everytime it goes off. Come on son, you'll have to come with me. I'm late. I don't know what they'll say when they see you but I'm bloody taking you to school by the ear. You hear me?'

She began rushing along the street, Nelson's sleeve in one hand, her carrier bag in the other. The boy had to run to keep from being dragged.

'Don't you dare try a trick like that again. Kidnapped, my arse. Nelson if I knew somebody who would kidnap you – I'd pay HIM the money. Embarrassing me on the street like that.'

They turned off the main road and went into a hallway and up carpeted stairs which had full-length mirrors along one side. Nelson stopped to make faces at himself but his mother chugged at his arm. At the head of the stairs stood a fat man in his shirtsleeves.

'What the hell is this?' ne said. 'You're late, and what the hell is that?' He looked down from over his stomach at Nelson.

'I'll explain later,' she said. 'I'll let him stay in the room.'

'You should be on NOW,' he said and turned and walked away through the swing doors. They followed him and Nelson saw, before his mother pushed him into the room, that it was a bar, plush and carpeted with crowds of men standing drinking.

'You sit here Nelson until I'm finished and then I'm taking you back to that school. You'll get nowhere if you don't do your lessons. I have to get changed now.'

She set her carrier bag on the floor and kicked off her

shoes. Nelson sat down watching her. She stopped and looked over her shoulder at him, biting her lip.

'Where's that bloody eyepatch you should be wearing?' Nelson indicated his pocket.

'Well wear it then.' Nelson took the crumpled patch from his pocket, tugging bits of it unstuck to get it flat before he stuck it over his bad eye. His mother took out her handbag and began rooting about at the bottom of it. Nelson heard the rattle of her bottles of scent and tubes of lipstick.

'Ah,' she said and produced another eyepatch, flicking it clean. 'Put another one on till I get changed. I don't want you noseying at me.' She came to him pulling away the white backing to the patch and stuck it over his remaining eye. He imagined that the tip of her tongue was stuck out, concentrating. When she spooned medicine into him *she* opened her mouth as well. She pressured his eyebrows with her thumbs, making sure that the patches were stuck.

'Now don't move or you'll bump into something.'

Nelson heard the slither of her clothes and her small grunts as she hurriedly got changed. Then he heard her rustle in her bag, the soft pop and rattle as she opened her capsules. Her 'tantalizers' she called them, small black and red torpedoes. Then he heard her voice.

'Just you stay like that till I come back. That way you'll come to no harm. You hear me Nelson? If I come back in here and you have those things off, I'll KILL you. I'll not be long.'

Nelson nodded from his darkness.

'The door will be locked so there's no running away.'

'Ah ken.'

Suddenly his darkness exploded with lights as he felt her bony hand strike his ear.

'You don't ken things, Nelson. You *know* them.'

He heard her go out and the key turn in the lock. His ear sang and he felt it was hot. He turned his face up to the ceiling. She had left the light on because he could see pinkish through the patches. He smelt the beer and stale smoke. Outside the room pop music had started up, very loudly. He heard the deep notes pound through to where he sat. He felt his ear with his hand and it *was* hot.

Making small aww sounds of excruciating pain, he slowly detached both eye-patches from the bridge of his nose outwards. In case his mother should come back he did not take them off completely, but left them hinged to the sides of his eyes. When he turned to look around him they flapped like blinkers.

It wasn't really a room, more a broom cupboard. Crates were stacked against one wall; brushes and mops and buckets stood near a very low sink; on a row of coat-hooks hung some limp raincoats and stained white jackets; his mother's stuff hung on the last hook. The floor was covered with tramped flat cork tips. Nelson got up to look at what he was sitting on. It was a crate of empties. He went to the keyhole and looked out but all he could see was a patch of wallpaper opposite. Above the door was a narrow window. He looked up at it, his eye-patches falling back to touch his ears. He went over to the sink and had a drink of water from the low tap, sucking in noisily at the column of water as it splashed into the sink. He stopped and wiped his mouth. The water felt cold after the mint of the chewing-gum. He looked up at his mother's things, hanging on the hook; her tights and drawers were as she wore them but inside out and hanging knock-kneed on top of everything. In her bag he found her blonde wig and tried it on, smelling the perfume of it as he did so. At home he liked noseying in his mother's room; smelling all her bottles of make-up; seeing her spangled things. He had to stand on the crate to see himself but the mirror was all brown measles under its surface and the eye-patches ruined the effect. He sat down again and began pulling at his chewing gum, seeing how long he could make it stretch before it broke. Still the music pounded outside. It was so loud the vibrations tickled his feet. He sighed and looked up at the window again.

If his mother took him back to school he could see problems. For starting St John the Baptist's she had bought him a brand new Adidas bag for his books. Over five pounds it had cost her, she said. On his first real skive he had dumped the bag in the bin at the bottom of his stair, every morning for a week and travelled light into town. On the Friday he came home just in time to see the bin lorry driving away in a cloud of bluish smoke. He had told his mother that the bag had been stolen from the playground during break. She had threatened to phone the school about it but Nelson had hastily assured her that the whole matter was being investigated by none other than the Headmaster himself. This threat put the notion out of his head of asking her for the money to replace the books. At that point he had not decided on a figure. He could maybe try it again sometime when all the fuss had died down. But now it was all going to be stirred if his mother took him to school.

He pulled two crates to the door and climbed up but it was not high enough. He put a third one on top and gingerly straightened, balancing on its rim. On tip-toe he could see out. He couldn't see his mother anywhere. He saw a crowd of men standing in a semi-circle. Behind them were some very bright lights, red, yellow and blue. They all had pints in their hands which they didn't seem to be drinking. They were all watching something which Nelson couldn't see. Suddenly the music stopped and the men all began drinking and talking. Standing on tip-toe for so long Nelson's legs began to shake and he heard the bottles in the crate rattle. He rested for a moment. Then the music started again. He looked to see. The men now just stood looking. It was as if they were seeing a ghost. Then they all cheered louder than the music.

Nelson climbed down and put the crates away from the door so that his mother could get in. He closed his eye-patches over for a while but still she didn't come. He listened to another record, this time a slow one. He decided to travel blind to get another drink of water. As he did so the music changed to fast. He heard the men cheering again, then the rattle of the key in the lock. Nelson, his arms rotating in front of him, tried to make his way back to the crate. His mother's voice said,

'Don't you dare take those eye-patches off.' Her voice was panting. Then his hand hit up against her. It was her bare stomach, hot and damp with sweat. She guided him to sit down, breathing heavily through her nose.

'I'll just get changed and then you're for school right away, boy.' Nelson nodded. He heard her light a cigarette as she dressed. When she had finished she ripped off his right eye-patch.

'There now, we're ready to go,' she said, ignoring Nelson's anguished yells.

'That's the wrong eye,' he said.

'Oh shit,' said his mother and ripped off the other one, turned it upside down and stuck it over his right eye. The smoke from the cigarette in her mouth trickled up into her eye and she held it half shut. Nelson could see the bright points of sweat shining through her make-up. She still hadn't got her breath back fully yet. She smelt of drink.

On the way out the fat man with the rolled up sleeves

held out two fivers and Nelson's mother put them into her purse.

'The boy – never again,' he said, looking down at Nelson.

They took the number twelve to St John the Baptist's. It was the worst possible time because, just as they were going in, the bell rang for the end of a period and suddenly the quad was full of pupils, all looking at Nelson and his mother. Some sixth-year boys wolf-whistled after her and others stopped to stare. Nelson felt a flush of pride that she was causing a stir. She was dressed in black satiny jeans, very tight, and her pink blouse was knotted, leaving her tanned midriff bare. They went into the office and a secretary came to the window.

'Yes?' she said, looking Mrs Skelly up and down.

'I'd like to see the Head,' she said.

'I'm afraid he's at a meeting. What is it about?'

'About him.' She waved her thumb over her shoulder at Nelson.

'What year is he?'

'What year are you, son?' His mother turned to him.

'First.'

'First Year. Oh then you'd best see Mr Mac Dermot, the First Year Housemaster.' The secretary directed them to Mr Mac Dermot's office. It was at the other side of the school and they had to walk what seemed miles of corridors before they found it. Mrs Skelly's stiletto heels clicked along the tiles.

'It's a wonder you don't get lost in here, son,' she said as she knocked on the Housemaster's door. Mr Mac Dermot opened it and invited them in. Nelson could see that he, too, was looking at her, his eyes wide and his face smiley.

'What can I do for you?' he said when they were seated.

'It's him,' said Mrs Skelly. 'He's been skiving again. I caught him this morning.'

'I see,' said Mr Mac Dermot. He was very young to be a Housemaster. He had a black moustache which he began to stroke with the back of his hand. He paused for a long time. Then he said,

'Remind me of your name, son.'

' – Oh I'm sorry,' said Mrs Skelly. 'My name is Skelly and this is my boy Nelson.'

'Ah yes Skelly.' The Housemaster got up and produced a yellow file from the filing cabinet. 'You must forgive me but we haven't seen a great deal of Nelson lately.'

'Do you mind if I smoke?' asked Mrs Skelly.

'Not at all,' said the Housemaster, getting up to open the window.

'The trouble is, that the last time we were at that Sub-attendance committee thing they said they would take court action if it happened again. And it has.'

'Well it may not come to that with the Attendance Sub-Committee. If we nip it in the bud. If Nelson makes an effort, isn't that right Nelson?' Nelson sat silent.

'Speak when the master's speaking to you,' yelled Mrs Skelly.

'Yes,' said Nelson, making it just barely audible.

'You're Irish too,' said Mrs Skelly to the Housemaster, smiling.

'That's right' said Mr Mac Dermot. 'I thought your accent was familiar. Where do you come from?'

'My family came from just outside Derry. And you?'

'Oh that's funny. I'm just across the border from you. Donegal.' As they talked Nelson stared out the window. He had never heard his mother so polite. He could just see a corner of the playing fields and a class coming out with the Gym teacher. Nelson hated Gym more than anything. It was crap. He loathed the changing rooms, the getting stripped in front of others, the stupidity he felt when he missed the ball. The smoke from his mother's cigarette went in an arc towards the open window. Distantly he could hear the class shouting as they started a game of football.

'Nelson! Isn't that right?' said Mr Mac Dermot loudly.

'What?'

'That even when you are here you don't work hard enough.'

'Hmm,' said Nelson.

'You don't have to tell me,' said his mother. 'It's not just his eye that's lazy. If you ask me the whole bloody lot of him is. I've never seen him washing a dish in his life and he leaves everything at his backside.'

'Yes,' said the Housemaster. Again he stroked his moustache. 'What is required from Nelson is a change of attitude. Attitude, Nelson. You understand a word like attitude?'

'Yes.'

'He's just not interested in school, Mrs Skelly.'

'I've no room to talk, of course. I had to leave at fifteen,' she said rolling her eyes in Nelson's direction. 'You know what I mean? Otherwise I might have staed on and got my exams.'

'I see,' said Mr Mac Dermot. 'Can we look forward to a change in attitude, Nelson?'

'Hm-hm.'

'Have you no friends in school?' asked the Housemaster.

'Naw.'

'And no interest. You see you can't be interested in any subject unless you do some work at it. Work pays dividends with interest . . .' he paused and looked at Mrs

Skelly. She was inhaling her cigarette. He went on, 'Have you considered the possibility that Nelson may be suffering from school phobia?'

Mrs Skelly looked at him. 'Phobia, my arse,' she said. 'He just doesn't like school.'

'I see. Does he do any work at home then?'

'Not since he had his bag with all his books in it stolen.'

'Stolen?'

Nelson leaned forward in his chair and said loudly and clearly, 'I'm going to try to be better from now on. I am. I am going to try, sir.'

'That's more like it,' said the Housemaster, also edging forward.

'I am not going to skive. I am going to try. Sir, I'm going to do my best.'

'Good boy. I think Mrs Skelly if I have a word with the right people and convey to them what we have spoken about, I think there will be no court action. Leave it with me, will you? And I'll see what I can do. Of course it all depends on Nelson. If he is as good as his word. One more truancy and I'll be forced to report it. And he must realize that he has three full years of school to do before he leaves us. You must be aware of my position in this matter. You understand what I'm saying, Nelson?'

'Ah ken,' he said. 'I know.'

'You go off to your class now. I have some more things to say to your mother.'

Nelson rose to his feet and shuffled towards the door. He stopped.

'Where do I go, sir?'

'Have you not got your time-table?'

'No sir. Lost it.'

The Housemaster, tut-tutting, dipped into another file, read a card and told him that he should be at R.K. in Room

72. As he left Nelson noticed that his mother had put her knee up against the Housemaster's desk and was swaying back in her chair, as she took out another cigarette.

'Bye love,' she said.

When he went into Room 72 there was a noise of oo's and ahh's from the others in the class. He said to the teacher that he had been seeing Mr Mac Dermot. She gave him a Bible and told him to sit down. He didn't know her name. He had her for English as well as R.K. She was always rabbiting on about poetry.

'You boy, that just came in. For your benefit we are talking and reading about organization. Page 667. About how we should divide our lives up with work and prayer. How we should put each part of the day to use, and each part of the year. This is one of the most beautiful passages in the whole of the Bible. Listen to its rhythms as I read.' She lightly drummed her closed fist on the desk in front of her.

'"There is an appointed time for everything, and a time for every affair under the heavens. A time to be born and a time to die; a time to plant and a time to uproot . . ."'

'What page did you say Miss?' asked Nelson.

'Six-six-seven,' she snapped and read on, her voice trembling. '"A time to kill and a time to heal; a time to wear down and a time to build. A time to weep and a time to laugh; a time to mourn and a time to dance . . ."'

Nelson looked out of the window, at the tiny white H of the goalposts in the distance. He took his chewing gum out and stuck it under the desk. The muscles of his jaw ached from chewing the now flavourless mass. He looked down at page 667 with its microscopic print, then put his face close to it. He tore off his eye-patch thinking that if he was going to become blind then the sooner it happened the better.

Three Resolutions to One Kashmiri Encounter

An Arid Title for a Human Incident

Giles Gordon

That morning I took a day tour in what was described in the brochure as a luxury coach from Srinagar – 'the russet-coloured, autumnal-smelling capital of Kashmir in the heady north of India' – to Gulmarg, 'the meadow of flowers', fifty-one kilometres away and 2590 metres up in the Himalayas.

The coach from Srinagar, a ravishing city built on water, as colourful and chaotic as its name is impossible to pronounce, passed through lush countryside. On both sides of the straight, well-surfaced roads were paddy fields – many of them saturated with water, being worked on more often than not by women of all ages in floral pyjama outfits, the female national dress of Kashmir – and avenues of poplars. High up in the mountains was snow which, even in the last week of April, defied all efforts by the blazing sun to dislodge it. From the distance, the white on the peaks looked glossy and sleek like the coats of well-tended ponies.

We stopped for a ten-minute break at Tangmarg, a mountain village and another beauty spot five and a half kilometres from the higher Gulmarg. I suspect the coach and its driver required a breather before undertaking the final ascent, the road from Tangmarg being narrow, circuitous and hazardous. I say 'final ascent' – final, that is, for vehicles, after which ponies and sledges, rope-tow and chair lift take over. The ski lifts were not in use, as on the lower slopes the snow had been melting for a couple of weeks, causing the rivers and streams to pour their brown and grey waters in torrents through the Kashmir valley. I didn't, at Tangmarg, avail myself of a cup of tea or coffee, as passengers were invited to do and most of the Indian families and couples did, preferring to wander up and down the single street of the village, looking at the bazaar and what through their open fronts the shops and stalls had to offer, and observe the mountain people. They were slim and wiry, taller and less stocky than the Nepalese, their faces without any spare flesh, tough, sun-beaten, snow-beaten: the countenance of a mountain people in the heart of Asia, further north than Tibet. They looked more Oriental than Indian. Visitors – five or six other coaches were parked in front of the Tourist Reception building in the middle of the village – mingled with the villagers. There was a whirl of activity. It was suddenly as if Tangmarg were a melting pot, the centre of the world. A stage had been animated.

A middle-aged man, with some distinction in his features and a dignified manner, was standing beside me, speaking to me. They tread so softly, so used are they to the terrain and the mountains, that you don't hear them approach. In good English – not at all with an Indian accent – he asked if I wouldn't prefer to leave the coach here and rejoin it on its return journey in the late afternoon, and he would guide me up the mountains, or wherever in the area I would like to go. I thanked him for his offer but declined.

'Only for six miles,' he said, and I was quietly pleased that he'd implied as great a mileage as that as being a short trek. He must have assumed I was more fit than I felt. The air up here made me tire easily and frequently search for breath. Again I declined, shaking my head.

'Let me come with you anyway,' he said, all the while absolutely and without difficulty managing to retain his character, individuality, dignity. There are beggars and beggars in India, indeed at times it seems both that they dominate the country and that the country has its being to enable them to beg, but not here in the exhilarating mountain air of Kashmir, gateway to heaven. There was, in this man, no element of grovelling, hardly even of importuning. He was his own master. His proposal was made entirely for my good. If I turned him down I was the loser.

'No, I prefer to go on my own,' I said. 'I'm sorry.' He seemed to accept my decision but showed no sign of being about to walk away, to solicit some other travellers. He began to tell me the names and heights of the local mountains, pointing them out to me, taking his time both as if to ensure I would manage to retain the information in my head and to prolong our encounter for its own sake. Besides, the *mountains* were hardly in a hurry. Harmukh and Ferozepur, Sunset Peaks and Apharwat Ridge. He kept the name and height of the last mountain, the mightiest of them all, to the end, producing it as if he'd just created the thing and I was the first to learn of his triumph: Nanga Parbat, 26,660 feet. How could I respond? Is *that* Nanga Parbat? Some height.

I said nothing, just looked. Still he stood by me, though it was as if I stood by him, as if I had sought him out and insisted on being with him. Somehow I felt it impossible – too discourteous to a fellow human being – to walk away from him. Besides, he might have followed me, though I didn't believe he would have done. And where could I have gone? Only up or down the village street, the street that was his village, his home. In my mind I urged the coach driver to sound his horn to indicate that we should all return to the vehicle, that it was about to move off and on to Gulmarg.

In a still, quiet voice – as if he was confiding in me – he began to talk again. 'Last year my wife died and I was left to bring up our three children. For six months one of them was in hospital, with a badly injured leg.' He paused, before going on. 'There is hardly any work here, in Tangmarg.'

I felt unable to say anything; or, rather, anything I might have said could only sound gratuitious, insensitive. He then said, so I understood it, that one rice meal a day for four people – and the children had big appetites – cost one rupee, which I'd have thought a little on the high side (a few pence) but hardly began to invalidate the point he was making. No work, no money, no food.

The horn of the coach went and I excused myself from him, saying that I hoped things got better for him, and quickly. I looked him in the eyes and nodded solemnly, as if to make it plain – in spite of having failed to provide him with employment and a rupee or two – that I wished him well. As if he could care. Somehow he managed neither to accept or acknowledge my farewell, my intended affirmation of good will in the face of the facts, nor to reject it. He allowed me to go.

Inside myself, I had panicked – for the sake of a coin or two – and felt disgusted. I was filled with a fluttering self-loathing. As the coach moved away, I watched him walking slowly down the street, his body built for survival, his head lowered a little in the direction of the ground.

Six hours later the coach returned. I'd prayed that it wouldn't halt at Tangmarg but it did, as in the morning on the way up. During the day, walking miles in the relentless and joyous air of the mountains, I found that my encounter with the man at Tangmarg kept coming back to me, nagged and fretted at the edges of my mind. Because I hadn't provided him with work, even for a short period of time, an hour or two, he had no money and therefore couldn't buy rice for his children and himself. On the other hand, so I tried to rationalize, I was hardly the only person he could have asked. There had been thirty or forty coaches at Gulmarg, and they all must have stopped at Tangmarg in the morning on the upward climb. I didn't owe the man a living, or no more than anyone else did. I wasn't his keeper. Our encounter had been a chance one. Why then should I have felt so strongly that I was the only person he asked, that because of that I was responsible for his well-being and that of his family? Had he not an obligation to go on asking people if they'd like to use his services until someone responded in the affirmative?

I remained in the overheated and airless coach at Tangmarg on the way back because I could see him from where the vehicle was parked, sitting on the ground in front of a shop, his hands wrapped around his raised knees. He didn't seem to belong to the shop, either to be working there or to be purchasing something from it. How could he have done, if he'd no money? Yet he seemed aware of the conversation going on between the man behind the counter and the person he was chatting to on the other side, in the street.

He looked no more hopeful or dejected than he had in the morning. It was as if the day had passed him by. He may have noticed my coach, realized that it was the one I arrived on in the morning, but he gave no indication of looking or of seeing, of being interested or concerned. Besides, most of these coaches looked pretty alike. He had troubled my mind but I doubted whether I had his, that my rejection of his services and of him had remained with him for longer than the moment of rejection had taken. The irony, of course, was that it was he who had wanted, needed something from me, not me from him.

Ten minutes later the coach started up, began to move from its parking place and down the hill on the last stage of its journey back to Srinagar. For as long as he was in view I watched from behind the curtain of my window seat. He didn't look up.

Six hours later, when the sun was beginning to descend towards and behind the mountains and what had been the excited, frenetic atmosphere of Gulmarg was growing wistful, contemplative, the coach began its return journey. As in the morning, on the way out, it stopped at Tangmarg. During the bright and crisp and peaceful hours of day, up above the valley, watching the men of the mountains pull visitors on sledges up snowy slopes and in and out of fir and pine forests, my meeting of the morning with the would-be guide of Tangmarg kept coming back to me, worrying at my mind. Especially did it do so when I was eating a skilfully cooked egg *paratha* and drinking a cup of steaming black tea at a refreshment hut high up in the mountains. It was an image, the meeting between us, which I couldn't with a clear conscience – with any conscience at all – expel from my mind. Had the man been sycophantically crawling, simply for alms (*baksheesh*, a tip or reward) as is the case with the majority of the beggars of India, then I would have had no compunction in not slipping him a coin. After all, he was able-bodied and thus able to work – eager to work. Both, I suspected, for the satisfaction of the work itself and for the income it would bring him. To have given him a rupee or two would have made no noticeable difference to my pocket. To him and his dependants it would have meant sustenance for a day or even two.

I alighted from the coach at Tangmarg with the other passengers but I didn't filter slowly into the café or to one of the tea stalls as most of them did. I looked about for my man, the man of the morning, having decided before arriving back that if he was in the street and I saw him I would give him two rupees. One which I should have given him in the morning, the other to appease my conscience.

I saw him almost as soon as I had stepped from the coach, coming up the street, in nearly the same place he'd been in in the morning when I saw him go down when the coach left. He wasn't looking up, he wasn't particularly looking up. He didn't give the impression of expecting to see someone he knew. Yet there was a kind of purposefulness about his progress, as if he wasn't proceeding up the street just to pass the time, to do something, that he wasn't walking merely for the sake of walking but that he had an objective in mind.

Though he was only a few paces from me, I began to move towards him. He looked up when I was close to him, three or four paces away, when he realized that someone was in his path. His eyes, which were both observant and bright yet somehow defeated, reconciled to the sorrows of life, of his life, registered no particular recognition of me; but neither the opposite. Our eyes met. I was neither stranger nor friend, enemy or ally.

'I wanted to thank you,' I said, 'for what you told me this morning.' The expression on his face didn't alter. 'About the mountains. Their names. Heights. Very interesting.'

I stopped. What more could I say, confronted with his silence, his lack of communication? I'd imagined he'd say something but he didn't. What could there have been for him to say? Yet he didn't seem to be judging me, despising me, which made it more difficult.

I held out my hand to him. His was raised to meet mine,

to take the money. Without looking down to see how much it was, he took the note, then withdrew his hand.

'Thank you,' he said; and then once more, as if he wasn't sure that he'd uttered the words the first time. There was a slow, grateful nod of the head before he broke away and walked around me and continued up the street to wherever he'd been going.

Six hours later, by the time the coach began its return journey to Srinagar, I had resolved upon a course of action. The day, for me, had been an unusually satisfying one. Unusually so, because I'm not regularly given to wandering about the snow-covered Himalayas. I'd had no preconceptions as to how I'd feel up there, higher than I'd ever been, how free and irresponsible yet somehow in command of my destiny. Close to, with the sun grinning down on their great flanks, the mountains looked as if hewn from marble. The local men, wearing multi-coloured knitted caps and woollen jumpers, dragged docile Indians on holiday up the slopes on sledges, into and amidst forests of vast firs. Children and sometimes adults pelted each other laboriously with snowballs, at times giggling solemnly as if Indians shouldn't indulge themselves as abandonedly as this. A red-turbaned Sikh thundered along a path on a white pony, followed at a proper distance by his wife and two daughters on grey ponies. On the lower levels the snow was melting fast, as if a whole winter's downpour felt obliged to vacate itself in one afternoon when confronted by incipient spring. Water flooded down springy, grassy fields translating them into water meadows. Huge black crows cackled and cawed, glided from tree to snow, snow to tree, black against white.

Against this heightened atmosphere – in both senses,

every sense – my unproductive (from his point of view) meeting with the man at Tangmarg in the morning lay at the back of my mind, tingeing my exultation in the present with irritation and dissatisfaction. Had the man begged, asked for alms, would I have given? After he'd told me his tale, assuming it was the same tale, I suspect I would. Not that, needing every coin and note and travellers' cheque I had with me in India, I'm in the habit of giving to beggars but because I believed the man implicitly, respected his self-respect and was grateful *not* to have him accompany me. I would have paid him so that I could be alone. All this, as I say, had he begged and importuned. But he didn't, he asked only to accompany me, to be my guide or companion for a period.

Near the end of the afternoon, before it was time to return to the coach, I had something tasty to eat and a glass of coffee with goat's milk at a café high up above the chair-lift wires. I took pleasure in watching the steam from the coffee rise upwards and look quite dark, almost opaque against the snow before turning translucent again and evaporating. Lurching downwards on the chair lift – above snow, trees, torrents of water, birds, people – I resolved what to do if the coach stopped at Tangmarg, as I felt pretty certain it would as Indians like their stops for tea or coffee. I even felt pleased with myself in anticipation.

As the coach parked in the centre of the village, the same spot as in the morning, alongside three other returning coaches, and with both villagers and visitors milling about, though without the excited tension, the expectancy of the morning, I at once saw my man. He was standing by a stall, a shop slightly down the sloping street from where the coach was. I hoped he wouldn't disappear before I could get out of the vehicle but, sitting near the back as I was, I was obliged to let the people in front alight first.

He was in the same place when I stepped out. I hurried over to him and stood there, smiling.

'Hallo,' I said.

'Sir,' he said, rather stiffly; 'sir', rather than the more usual 'sahib'.

I felt slightly hurt that he wasn't immediately more forthcoming, more friendly. *Presumably* he recognized me, remembered.

'Look,' I said, 'I'd like you to have this,' and held out to him the five-rupee note which I'd been clutching in my hand for half an hour or more. He looked down at it.

'No, sir,' he said, peering into my eyes. 'I asked you this morning if you'd employ me, and you wouldn't.' Then, without a pause: 'How did you like Gulmarg?'

'I . . . liked it . . . a lot,' I said, well aware of the feebleness of my response in the face of his rejection of my money, and of me.

'Yes, it is very beautiful,' he said.

'Very beautiful,' I repeated.

He walked away, up the street. Slowly I returned to the coach, crushing the note in my hand. There was little point in hurrying as the vehicle wouldn't be leaving until everyone had had their tea or coffee.

'To Autumn', by Ernest Lovejoy

Brian McCabe

It was an ordinary October day in Edinburgh, the rain more or less incessant. Ernest Lovejoy – an unsmiling, unmarried and widely unpublished poet – was on his way home from his job in the public library when he realized that autumn had been underway for over a fortnight, and still no poem. His rain-stung fingers clenched around the polythene carrier-bag, which contained this week's ration of literature alongside the ingredients of a solitary bolognaise. Normally he'd have a sonnet on the go by now. Or, if he felt experimental, a *vers libre* 'Autumn', or even a sequence of haikus. At the very least, a prosepoem.

Last year – he gazed at the ground as he remembered it and saw, beneath his feet, all the motley leaves stuck to the wet stone like . . . *like* – he'd turned his hand to a very modern, almost concrete 'Autumn', in which a zigzagging arrangement of fragmented lines had been meant to suggest, mimetically, the leaves falling from the trees. No one could accuse him of being old-fashioned or unoriginal in *that* poem, though he would of course be willing to acknowledge the influences of Apollinaire, Dylan Thomas, e.e. cummings and possibly Lewis Carroll if the critics insisted. Those spiralling line-arrangements had been hell to type out – Lovejoy's typewriter was as old as Lovejoy, and just as temperamental – and then there had been all the problems involved in composing a suitably modern, up-to-date description of the season's change, taking great care of course to avoid all mention of trees. Each time he'd sent out that particular celebration of the earth's rhythm – four times, all told, then winter had set in – it had come back almost by return of post. A leaf determined to fall, with the editor's seasonal regrets.

Lovejoy grimaced at the ground – all those windblown, amber-bronze-golden leaves swirling round his feet like a . . . *like a* – as he recalled the remark one editor had thought him worthy of: *Promising. But too many similes, and too much alliteration.* Hadn't the man read Keats? And at Lovejoy's age – he was thirty-five, and keen on Conrad – that 'promising' had long since ceased to console. And now it was here again, season of mists and rejectionslips, just begging to be quatrained.

With his free hand he tugged the lapels of his jacket together, cursing the weather under his breath. With every step, the rain seeped up through his cracked soles, and every time he took a breath the icy wind did something onomatopoeic between his teeth. As he passed by a bookshop he slowed down and hesitated outside the door. The feeling of wanting to be inside, but at the same time the reluctance to enter. Not that he didn't have money to spare on a book – it was something worse than that. The pleasure Lovejoy took in browsing had palled, recently. Instead a strange sense of disgust, the word was not too strong, when confronted by all those regimented classics and those squadrons of paperback novels. Oddly enough this had not affected his work. The books in the library were, after all, only items to be numbered, catalogued and dusted. The ones on sale were somehow different, so much more challenging. Even the poetry section, with its slim and elegant editions of the living and its fat, complete works of the dead, no longer offered Lovejoy consolation. At first he had told himself that he was appalled by the way literature had become so much a commodity – all those box-sets of Jane Austen and portable Hemingways for God's sake – but he knew that it was more than this. He knew that he was beginning to feel a keen despair with himself: with so much of the stuff already on the market, what could he, E. Lovejoy, hope to add?

A sequence of sonnets would be the thing. Establish himself with the traditional, the exciting new departures could come later.

Staring at the window display of best-sellers, Lovejoy caught sight of his reflection in the glass: too thin to be called slim, spineless in any case. The jacket plain, dogeared. The frontspiece of his face perhaps a reproduction of a print by Eduard Munch. Clearly destined to remain on the shelf, a book never to be reviewed. A limited edition of one.

He turned away from the bookshop – perhaps posterity would discover his manuscripts – and decided despite the weather and the hollow pain in his stomach to take the long way home through the park. Perhaps that small expanse of grass and sky, while barred clouds bloom the soft-dying etcetera, would spark off something. A couplet, maybe. Then he'd have something to work on after the spaghetti. This thought put a bounce into Lovejoy's step – his feet couldn't get much wetter – as he crossed the road and headed for the park. By the time its gates were in sight, he was already at work on it. Not the first draft perhaps, but very possibly the one *before* that, the one in the mind. His lips mimed the round-vowelled sounds which would soon become the syllables, then the words and the lines of the poem which, unless he was fooling himself, was very much immanent: 'To Autumn', by Ernest Lovejoy.

*   *   *

Maybe he was trying too hard.

More than half-an-hour had passed, slowly, with Lovejoy huddled in the shelter of the cricket pavilion, notebook in hand. Staring out at the rain there swaying in the rain, a thin veil over autumn's elusive face. Raindrops lining the roof's edge the beads of her endless necklace. But nothing had come, not a word. The drab, dilapidated pavilion, daubed with gaudily painted gang-names, was beginning to depress him. Unfortunately it wasn't the right kind of depression, the kind which – he'd often heard it said – brought with it a muse. This was no such solemn, dignified emotion. This was an ordinary feeling of depression, a mere feeling of lack. What he needed was a good meta-phor. He stared at a long line of cars passing along the road outside the park. How slowly, how monotonously those cars followed one another along, like the days of Lovejoy's life. He leaned back against the wall and closed his eyes and listened for the poem inside. The wind went on incanting her thin, meaningless vowel. The rain went on whispering her narrative on the roof.

No words came to Lovejoy.

Dropping the notebook and the pen, Lovejoy stood up and leaned against the wooden balustrade of the pavilion. He peered at a nearby tree. A tiny, bright red leaf came loose from a branch and was blown quickly towards him, landing a few inches from his foot. There was nothing very moving about the process as far as Lovejoy could see, if anything it looked slightly comical. If it made him feel anything at all, it wasn't the exquisite melancholy we associate with the perception of transience. He felt wet, and depressed, and ridiculous. As if through this so written-about phenomenon they called 'autumn', something or someone were poking fun at him. He had to concentrate, be serious.

What he needed was a personification.

Even the wind was distracting him from the task in hand. Running berserk among the shrubs like that. It wasn't exactly winnowing anyway. More like grabbing the trees by their throats and trying to throttle them. Picking up all the sodden leaves and throwing them around like that, like a lunatic. Suddenly Lovejoy sat down and picked up the notebook and the pen. He began to write furiously, words both momentous and illegible:

Wild wind, like a lunatic let loose –

For a moment he didn't quite know how to go on, but still. Quite a beginning. One more syllable and it might be the first line of a sonnet. He'd have to sort out the pentameters of course, get the thing to scan here and there. It was a fresh personification though, what with autumn as an escaped lunatic. All sorts of possibilities began to crowd into his mind. Winter as a group of male nurses, their icy eyes closing in on Autumn in the sestet somewhere. Lovejoy looked at the first line with dazed, admiring eyes. Then he heard, in the recesses of his consciousness, a small editorial voice: *Too many similes, and too much alliteration.*

'Hi there!'

Lovejoy closed the notebook with haste as he looked up. The girl – she looked like a student – swung her rucksack down beside him and began unbuckling the flap.

'Gee-zus, what rain! I'm *soaked*,' said the girl.

'It really is ah . . . raining, isn't it?' said Lovejoy, tucking the notebook into his jacket pocket.

'Raining! Man, it's *the Flood*.'

'Sometimes it's much worse than this here. During the winter it's – '

'If it gets any worse we'll need *snorkels*. Holy shit, it's like *Venice* without the *gondolas*. You waiting for the life-boat here, or what? Hey, you got a bottle?'

'Bottle? No, I – '

'Pity. I figured we could maybe send a message out, I mean like an s.o.s.'

Lovejoy watched in silence as she tugged a brown towel from her rucksack and began to dry her hair. She wore a maroon jerkin, a tight-fitting orange sweatshirt, brown corduroy jeans and a pair of beige leather boots. She was small, good-looking and there wasn't anything wrong with her. As his glances strayed from her face and hair to her shoulders and breasts, then down to her neat waist and hips, the word which came to Lovejoy's mind was *regular*. The only irregular thing about her seemed to be her eyes, which were green and very wide open, but which squinted a little. Perhaps it was the cat-like eyes which filled Lovejoy with hopeless longing. Or perhaps it was just that she was a regular American girl, come to him now in his hour of need, in the autumn of his youth, bearing the gift Lovejoy needed more than anything: words. He was aware that from time to time those green eyes were glancing at him between the dark hair and the towel. She expected him to say something more. Something interesting. They'd already covered the weather, and he sensed that to engage her for any length of time – a drink was already in his mind, then perhaps a candle-lit bolognaise for two – he'd have to impress her somehow.

The rain told its story on the roof, no words came to Lovejoy.

She threw the towel down on the top of her rucksack, sat down on the wooden floor, shuddered with the cold and pulled a packet of *Lucky Strike* from her jerkin pocket.

'You're ah . . . from America?' said Lovejoy. It wasn't much of a beginning, but perhaps the rest would follow from the first line. She nodded, lighting a cigarette, apparently waiting for him to continue. But in his mind Lovejoy was furiously scoring out that dull first line. That was the trouble with life, you couldn't revise it:

'Which part of the ah . . . States are you from?'

'I'm from Providence Rhode Island. My name's Louise, what's yours?'

'Ernest,' said Lovejoy.

'As in Hemingway, huh?' said Louise, squinting mischievously. 'Well hi Ernest, would you like a cigarette?'

'Please,' said Lovejoy, 'Thanks.' As he took the cigarette, he glanced again at those eyes. It wasn't just the squint which made them unusual, but also the staring quality they had – wide open not with innocence or surprise but something much more permanent, and durable. When she offered him a light, he wanted to steady her hand – not that it was unsteady, but it would be a touch, a trust – but his own hand somehow declined to make the contact. As always with Lovejoy, regrets were coming before the act. He thanked her again, inhaled deeply and gazed out over the park. He searched among the windblown leaves for his next line.

'Autumn,' he said, motioning loosely with a hand to the rain, the earth and the sky, 'always makes me feel a bit ah . . . melancholic.'

'Check,' said Louise. She blew a smoke-ring from her small mouth and added: 'I guess I interrupted you, huh?'

Lovejoy looked puzzled.

'Weren't you writing when I came along?'

'Oh, *that*,' said Lovejoy. He tried to smile nonchalantly. 'I was trying to.'

'You go right ahead and write,' said Louise, pointing

with the lit tip of her cigarette to Lovejoy's jacket pocket.
'No shit, I won't disturb you.'

'It's all right, really, I don't want to.'

'You want me to go away?'

'O no! I mean actually, well, as a matter of fact . . . I
wasn't getting on too well with it.'

The green eyes stared at him squintly and with an
intensity Lovejoy found unsettling.

'You a writer?'

This question had always brought a dilemma for
Lovejoy. If he said yes, the next question would almost
certainly concern his publisher. If no, he'd have to own up
to his job in the library – hardly the sort of occupation to
enthral this girl from Providence Rhode Island, with her
challenging green eyes, her *Lucky Strike*, her 'gee-zus'
and 'holy shit'. Lovejoy therefore tried to sidestep the
issue, nodding in a non-committal way, tilting his head a
little to the side.

'You are?'

'Yes.'

'Who d'you write for?'

'Posterity.'

'I don't think I know it.'

Louise blowing smoke into the face of this late autumn
afternoon, the separate stares of her wide green eyes
meeting on Lovejoy's mouth. Lovejoy still nervous about
the question: to be a writer or not to be a writer. He had
to change the subject fast:

'Are you ah . . . on holiday here?'

Louise cleared her throat, flicked her ash and licked her
neat red lips with the tip of her tongue. Lovejoy looked
away, over the park to the queueing cars, unable to bear
the desire that this peeping tongue aroused.

'Kinda,' said Louise. 'Kinda convalescing. See I was at

Brown – that's the University in Providence. You heard of it? – and I was in my final semester, right? And wow, well it's a long story but I had this affair with my tutor. Okay okay, I know what you're thinking. You're thinking I'm *stoopid*, right? It was stoopid, the whole thing was all so *stoopid*. But when it happens it happens, right, so I fell in love with the creep. Boy, was he a creep. Turned out to be a mean little shit. O he was very *distinguished*. *Learned*, and all that crap. And very *respected* of course, by everyone including me till I realized what a *jerk* he was. He was a *writer* too, I even read all of his *books*! Anyway it didn't work out, of course – he was old enough to be my father, for Christ's sake – and so it fell apart. We didn't really have much in common I guess, except sex I guess. We *could* have, I really believe we coulda given each other a whole lot more, you know what I mean, but when it came down to it he didn't *wanna* have anything else in common. So all we did was fuck like snakes, till one day his *wife* found a tube of *ortho-cream* in the car. Don't get the wrong idea, we didn't actually *do* it in the *car* – it musta fallen outa my *bag* I guess. I wouldn't 've minded so much if she'd found a *love letter* or something, but *ortho-cream* of all the shitty things. So she knew it wasn't *hers*, 'cause she'd been *sterilized* years ago. It made me feel kinda cheap. Just something to fuck if you know what I mean, something to *fuck* between his *seminars*, between chapter eight and chapter nine of his latest shitty *book*. That's what I was, I can see it now. Anyhow, in the end he went to his little wifeling with his little tail between his legs, promised *never* to be a *naughty* little professor *again*. And then they threw away that *nasty*, *horrible* tube of contraceptive jelly and lived happily ever after. The end. Meanwhile I went crazy. No kidding, the whole thing screwed me up so much I flunked my exams. Overdose, the whole scene. Made a shitty mess of *that* too. I took a year out and went to see an analyst, some jungian nut with big hairy hands he kept *pawing* me with. Worked a coupla months in the library there in Providence, but shit was it boring, you know?'

'I know,' said Lovejoy.

'Heaving all those *books* around, boy that was *death*. Holy shit, you know what I used to do? I used to turn *his* books around, with the spines turned in so I couldn't even see the creep's *name*. That's how scewed up *I* was. So I quit, went to Italy and France. Then a coupla weeks in London. Caught a train up here. I'm going up north tomorrow. I guess I'll catch a train to Glasgow first, then head up there to the islands. Anyway here I am telling you my life story and drowning in this Scottish rain. So what d'you write anyway, Ernest? You a journalist?'

'O no,' said Lovejoy, still trying to assimilate the wealth of emotional data she had unpacked. 'No I write ah – ' He had never been able to say it with complete nonchalance. Either it came out sounding pretentious, an extravagant lie, or as if it might refer to something unwholesome, something a grown man ought to keep under his hat. But there was no way round it: 'Poetry.'

In his mouth the word sounded more unfamiliar than ever, and faintly obscene.

'What kinda poetry?'

A difficult question for Lovejoy, he wrote so many kinds of the stuff. He leaned forward, elbows on knees, and stared at the ground. A mob of literary terms crowded into his mind, each shouting for his attention. He caught sight of the tiny red leaf the wind had blown to him earlier. He picked it up and held it between his fingers. What kind of poetry.

'Mostly the unpublished kind.'

To his immense relief, she laughed. What neat, regular little teeth. It wasn't much of a laugh, not quite a guffaw. But a little laugh was better than no laugh at all. Louise stubbed out her cigarette and laughed again.

'Hey, that's the *same kind* I write!'

Lovejoy managed a laugh too. Suddenly Ernest and Louise, the unpublished poets, had made contact through humour. As if to put this on record, they laughed again, this time in unison. When they had finished there was a new kind of silence between them. One they could share and relax with.

'Look at this,' said Lovejoy, holding out the scarlet, almost heart-shaped leaf in his palm. Louise leaned closer and picked the leaf out of his palm. Her green sphinxy eyes scrutinized it closely, then looked up.

'Mmm,' she said, 'it's neat.'

Things were looking neat for Lovejoy.

While he was in the bedroom, Lovejoy took the opportunity to make the bed. From time to time he stopped and stared for a moment at nothing, as if dazed. Was this really happening to *him*? Yes, it was. He was falling – not madly perhaps, and not without a sense of the folly of it, but falling all the same and grateful for it – in love with this green-eyed Louise. Finishing off the bed, he pulled his notebooks and folders from the drawer of his writing desk. He began to look through them. He wondered how he was doing – had she liked the meal? She had described it as sedating. Still, the conversation had gone quite well, and already in the living room the lights were low, the music soft. Lovejoy felt mellow, relaxed. The bottle of red wine Louise had bought on the way to the flat had certainly helped. After the meal, Louise had read some of her poems, all of which seemed to be addressed to the creep of a professor. She had asked him to read a few of his, and he had agreed. Leafing through the badly typed pages, he now wondered if this was such a good idea. Still, he'd come clean about his job and it hadn't made her jump up and call a taxi. If anything it had helped things along a little – it was, after all, something they had in common – but Lovejoy now wished he had steered the conversation away from literature, especially his, and had kept it on the subject of sexual relationships, especially hers. What she had to say in that area intrigued him deeply, since his own experience of love-making had never involved a water-bed, a perineum – whatever *that* was – or the application of coconut oil.

He had never tried it the American way.

Collecting together the poems he'd picked out, Lovejoy consulted his image in the wardrobe mirror. Though his thinning hair had dried out, it still lay flat against his skull. His pink scalp shone through the gaps between the hair, which clung mainly to the sides of his head. He tousled it up, and returned to the living room. Louise had thoughtfully arranged a few cushions on the floor near the electric fire. Albinoni's violins wept from the stereo, and generally the room had an atmosphere Lovejoy had never been able to create on his own.

'Mind if I roll one?' said Louise. He noticed that she had in her hand a polythene bag filled with dried leaves.

'What is it?' said Lovejoy. He sat down awkwardly on the cushions and peered at the bag of leaves.

'Colombian,' said Louise. 'It's good.'

Lovejoy shrugged, smiled and nodded all at once. Though he'd heard of it of course, and had sometimes caught its aroma at parties, he'd never actually tried it. Still, he didn't wish to appear old-fashioned or stuffy.

Anyway, what the hell, he was in the mood for a new experience.

'Are you sure you ah . . . want me to *read* them?' he said. 'You could look at one or two yourself.'

'I'd like it oral,' said Louise, rolling the dark grass into a long paper printed with a tiny version of the stars and stripes. Lovejoy watched, enchanted by the inch of tongue with which she licked its gummed edge.

'Aren't you going to ah . . . put some tobacco in too?'

'You read the poems, I'll roll the sticks. Okay?'

Lovejoy nodded and shuffled through his pages. He pulled out one and looked it over, biting his lip.

'I suppose I could read this one, if you like.'

'What's its name?' Louise lit the American flag fat with leaves and passed it to Lovejoy.

'Autumn in the City,' said Lovejoy.

'Shoot.'

He cleared his throat, reannounced the title, then took a few deep inhalations of the sweetly smelling smoke. To begin with he read the lines nervously and too quickly. He had never read anything aloud like this before. Soon, however, his own voice seemed to swell and resonate around the words. The words themselves seemed to be charged with a power he had not suspected of them, and there was nothing for it but to let the words take over. Between poems Louise said nothing, but passed him the long smoking thing and urged him to read the next. After a time, she lay back on the cushions, closed her eyes and apparently let the words take over too. Lovejoy went on reciting, his voice rich with implication. Suddenly, half way through a quatrain, something strange began to happen. He no longer understood the words. Their sounds became ominous, and ridiculous, and all sorts of other things. It was as if their history, the sum total of their usages and associations, had become somehow actual and present as he uttered them. They danced along the page before his eyes, a cryptic script he could no longer decipher, an algebra of lyricism he could barely remember how to pronounce. He did not understand, either, why he had written all this down in the first place, nor why he was now reading it aloud to a stranger who appeared to be falling asleep on the living-room floor. He stumbled, faltered and stopped on the word 'now'.

After a moment Louise stirred, opened her eyes and yawned.

'Mmm,' she said, 'you wanna know what I think? I think it's got a lotta potential, but . . . You wanna know what it reminds me of?'

'Keats,' said Lovejoy abstractedly.

'Well, yeah. A lotta stuff about the fall. And that one about the nymph, that nymph in the garden, you know. I guess that was kinda Keatsian.'

'Did you think there was too much ah . . . simile? Alliteration?' said Lovejoy, still intrigued and slightly alarmed by the sound and the power of each word as he uttered it.

'Maybe there was, yeah. But you wanna know what it reminded me of? My father. See I was never too close to my father, I guess. It's a long story but anyway, he was an alcoholic. Boy, was he an alcoholic. Anyhow, I never really felt I had a father. He was always leaving or going in somewhere to dry out, you know? So I guess I didn't see too much of him. Even when I did see him, he wasn't *there*, if you see what I mean. He was somewhere else. Which is why I probably got stuck on that *jerk* of a professor. I guess I kinda needed a surrogate. Anyhow, my father painted pictures, right, he was an artist or so he thought. A few other people thought he was too, so they bought his pictures. Which was the worst thing they coulda done, if you ask me. Anyway, your poems kinda reminded me of my father's pictures, you know? 'Cause every one is like it's been written by a different person, sort of. I mean, you walk into my mother's apartment and it's like the History of Art, volumes one to twenty. Giotto to Jackson Pollock, the whole caboodle. Cubism, fauvism, expressionism, every stoopid old ism you can think of. It's all there on the walls, every style and technique there is. Everything except him, you know?'

'I know,' said Lovejoy sadly.

'You do?'

'Sure,' said Lovejoy, surprised a little by his own use of the word, 'you mean none are genuine. None of your father's paintings, and none of my ah . . . poems.'

'Well, I wouldn't say *that*,' said Louise, propping herself up on one elbow and opening her eyes full. 'Don't get me wrong, I'm not trying to be critical or anything. I liked some and I wasn't so keen on some others, but mostly they just kinda reminded me of a whole lotta other poems. I mean there's nothing *wrong* with that. You gotta have some influences, but you've gotta find your own kinda – '

'I never have,' said Lovejoy, and the words seemed to well from a deeper source than the one which had given rise to his poetry.

'You *will*,' said Louise, 'if you really want to.'

He knew that normally he would find such an appraisal wounding. Tonight he wanted to hear it, the truth. He smiled, then giggled a little. Louise responded by smiling back at him. Lovejoy laughed out loud. Inside, he felt a peculiar radiance spreading through his limbs, as if his cells were alight, as if somewhere inside him a younger, more agile, and much stronger man were stretching, rippling and getting ready to come out. Perhaps it was this inner man who stretched out a hand and ran a finger down the side of Louise's face, lightly stroked her neck, her shoulder, her breast.

Louise whispering something in his ear about a cap, her mouth so close to his ear that the words become a caress.

Lovejoy awoke to the abrupt noise of the front door closing. He felt groggy, and as if he had aged considerably during the night. He coughed harshly, then gulped down the bitter phlegm. What variety of passions he had partaken of, what inventive intimacies, what prolonged pleasures with Louise. But where was Louise? Had she gone without a goodbye?

He stumbled out of bed and, noticing the clock, realized that he was hopelessly late for work. But this was not the point, the point was Louise. He staggered to the window and caught sight of her, pack on her back, dark hair blown back by the wind, turning the corner out of the street. Perhaps he could catch her, if he hurried? But then, what would be the point? She had decided to go. He stood by the window for a few moments, staring absently at the sunlight flashing from a puddle of dirty water. Was this what a poet would call sweet sorrow? In any case he felt it keenly, but also felt a pressing need to piss. Naked, Lovejoy walked to the toilet and listened with closed eyes to the rattle of his water in the bowl.

In the living room he found her note, propped up against the empty wine bottle:

Dear Ernest,
Tried to wake you up, but I guess you'd gone into hibernation for the winter. Hope you don't hate me for running off like this, I decided to go book a flight. I figure I'll do my final year again when I get back, get myself straightened out. Maybe see you

*again sometime – who knows, maybe I'll visit Scotland again next
fall. Everything changes, I guess.*

>*See ya,*
>>*crazy Louise.*
>>>*X X X*

P.S. You gotta keep on writing, Ernest. Start with this.

A long arrow trailing down to the bottom of the note.
On the table lay the tiny, scarlet leaf. Lovejoy picked it up
and stared at it in wonder, confounded by its tiny shape,
its tiny colour, and by the feel of its tiny flesh between his
fingers, unlike anything else in the world.

The German Boy

Ron Butlin

The woman I can see standing outside in the pouring rain reminds me of Klaus, the German boy. It is the expression on her face: she looks . . . so desolate, so utterly unloved. People hurry past her as quickly as possible; if someone does smile, I watch her hesitate for a moment. Then she looks away.

When I came to the office about half-an-hour ago I passed her by pretending interest in a shop-display. From here, however, I can study her in perfect safety. Perhaps she is waiting for someone. I realize now that she could not have been taken in by my elaborate charade for it is repeated every few minutes by others – repeated too frequently to be convincing. At one time I might have pitied her, for that kind of cruelty comes easiest of all. Believe me, I know – Klaus taught me that.

This morning I have come to the office and done nothing. There is a pile of correspondence for me, some of it marked 'urgent'. Instead I stand and stare out of the window at the well-dressed woman opposite. She is in her mid-forties. I think she is crying but it is difficult to tell at this distance. She has glanced in my direction so I will move back from the window.

I remember my headmaster talking to us before Klaus was brought in.

'There is nothing special about him,' he said. 'Remember, he is just like the rest of us.'

When he came into the classroom for the first time, however, it was quite obvious he was not like the rest of us: Klaus looked different, he talked different and, even though he wore the same clothes as us, somehow he seemed to be dressed differently. Everyone looked at him and he looked at the floor. He had fair hair, very pale skin and was quite tall. His shoulders were trembling – an action his long arms increased proportionally, making his hands jerk as if they were receiving a series of small electric shocks.

'This is Klaus, he is going to join your class.' The headmaster was a small red-faced man who always looked as if he was too small and too red-faced to be comfortable. When he died a few months later from sunstroke I imagined him as having simply exploded one very hot afternoon.

My family talked a great deal about 'class' which for a long time I confused with my schoolfriends who were all of one class in both senses of the word. 'He is of a different class altogether' meant, to me, that someone was simply a few years older or younger than myself. And when my Aunt Claire happened to remark during an Open Day that Klaus was of a different class to the rest of the boys, I hastened to correct her saying that on the contrary he was the same age as myself and we sat next to each other and were the very best of friends. She said I was a very kind and thoughtful boy; and I replied excitedly that I was going to learn German. 'Of course you should help him to be at his ease, but you mustn't neglect your proper studies,' she concluded with a smile.

Klaus didn't even glance at the class he was about to join. He looked more uncomfortable than ever: his knees began shaking and his hands, in an effort to control the effects of the 'electric shocks', had grasped his jacket tightly at the sides – which served only to increase his nervous jerkings by the amount of 'give' in the material.

The headmaster ushered him to one side of a map of the world which had the British Empire coloured red, 'an unfortunate choice of colour' my aunt had observed during her visit. Then he indicated Germany and spoke to Klaus in German: he replied, '*Ja, mein Herr*' without raising his eyes from the floor. And then a moment later he did look up – not at the map, however, but at us; and he smiled, then blushed and returned his gaze to the floor. A boy sniggered. The headmaster plodded on.

'Klaus is from Germany. This is Germany.' He indicated it again. ' – *Deutschland*.' He smiled at Klaus then looked at us once more.

'*Deutschland* – that's "Germany" in German. Now, does anyone here speak German?' The boy who had sniggered before shouted out, '*Ja, mein Herr*' making us all laugh.

Klaus sat next to me. He didn't speak English but we managed somehow in Latin. He told me he had been born and brought up in Germany but when his father died his mother had married an Englishman. He had only been here a week but he liked it. He said that he and I were friends – *amici sumus*. That was nearly twenty years ago.

I really should get down to some work. Normally I work hard, very hard. In the name of Cochrane and Assocs. I deal in money: I buy it, sell it, lend it. I deal only with certain people and in private. They have confidence in me. They assume that having maintained credibility in the past, then our house will do so in the future – and perhaps they are right, for as long as they trust us then we can do business and so justify that trust. In the course of time I am expected to become head of the firm. I would have liked that.

P.B.S.S.S.–H

When I was a child our family was well-off. There was an inheritance which my father employed wisely. I attended public school before going up to Oxford to read Classics. I was hard-working rather than brilliant. My father died when I was in my third year and I returned home immediately, to be told that he had committed suicide. We were completely bankrupt. Everything had to be sold; I had to leave Oxford and begin working in the City. For the last ten years I have worked hard to restore the family name.

Last night we had a special dinner, Sylvia and I, to celebrate our wedding anniversary – we have been married for five years. Afterwards she said she was proud of me as a husband, lover and merchant banker. She kissed me.

Recently I have had occasion to go over our company books and it has become apparent to me that our business methods are as hopelessly out-of-date as our furniture and fittings; and with our present commitments it is too late to correct the situation. We will be finished by the end of the year. Strictly speaking we are finished already but as yet no one else knows. However, once word gets around the City, we will have to shut-up shop: for a company that is failing, especially an old company, may inspire pity – but never investment. I want to tell my wife. I want to tell my partners.

Instead I say nothing. I stand at my office window staring out into the street at a complete stranger standing in the pouring rain. She has hardly moved from where I first saw her. She must be soaked through and very cold now. She appears very unhappy – I would like to go over and speak to her, to say 'Don't worry' or something like that; or perhaps even to smile at her from here. I would like to, but I know I won't.

On his first night in our dormitory Klaus was given the

bed next to mine and I could hear him crying. The room
was in darkness but I could just make him out under the
blankets. He was kneeling and bending forwards with his
head pushing into the pillow.

'Klaus, Klaus,' I called in a low voice. Quietly I went
over to him and sat on his bed.

'Don't cry, don't cry. You're here now. It will be good –
you and me together. Honest.'

He made some reply in a voice muffled as much by his
tears as by the blankets. He probably hadn't understood a
word I had said. I sat with him for nearly half-an-hour
while he cried, then I went back to bed. The next night
was the same, and every night afterwards. During the day
he was fine: he worked hard in class and joined in the
games. Gradually his English improved. Each night,
however, he cried himself to sleep. Then one day, during
the morning break, he told me that from then on he was
going to speak only in German – except to me, of course.
At first I thought he was joking, but he wasn't.

The next class was arithmetic and near the end of the
lesson our teacher began going over the problems out
loud.

'Klaus, No. 4 please, the one about the reservoir.'
Klaus stood up to give his answer. He seemed uncertain
and he mumbled. The teacher asked him to repeat it. He
spoke more clearly this time: '*Zwei Minuten.*' The class
laughed and even the teacher joined in a little before
asking him to repeat it in English.

'*Zwei Minuten.*' The class laughed even louder, but this
time the teacher didn't even smile.

'In English, Klaus, if you please,' he said quite firmly.

'*Zwei Minuten,*' Klaus repeated; his fingers were gripping the sides of the desk-lid and his body shook. The
teacher asked him again, and again the class went into

uproar at his reply. His face was white. He was gripping the desk so tightly it rattled against the floor. He began repeating his answer: '*Zwei Minuten Zwei Minuten Zwei Minuten* . . .' He was staring ahead, quite oblivious to the noise about him.

The teacher didn't know what to do . . . He told Klaus to sit down and he wouldn't. To be quiet and he wouldn't. To stand in the corner and he wouldn't. '*Zwei Minuten Zwei Minuten* . . .' Tears were running down his cheeks and his voice was choking but he couldn't stop. Finally he was taken to the sick-room.

He came back afterwards but still refused to speak English. A few days later he was sent home. I have never seen him since and hardly even given him a moment's thought until now.

It has stopped raining. The woman is still waiting there but in the sunlight, she looks less miserable. She has been there for forty minutes now, at least.

To work. I suppose I have to fill up the day somehow and then return home. And I will have to think how to tell Sylvia that the business is collapsing.

She will have cooked dinner for my arrival tonight and we will eat together with the children. Afterwards I will read them a bedtime story, then we will probably watch TV. A few hours later it will be time to go to bed – and still I will not have told her.

And tomorrow I will return to the office; and the day after. There will be letters marked 'urgent', cables, meetings, luncheons, delicate negotiations and so forth. And every evening I will return home to Sylvia. Back and forwards; back and forwards I will go saying nothing.

The woman has turned to check her appearance in the shop-window. She is adjusting her hat. I watch as she crosses the road and now walks quickly past my window and down the street.

I have sat down in my executive leather chair. At any moment the telephone may ring or my secretary announce someone to see me – until then I will do nothing except rest my feet on the desk. For how long? I wonder.

'*Zwei Minuten Zwei Minuten* . . .' I hear Klaus say – which I now understand as meaning a lifetime, or as good as.

The Care and Attention of Swimming Pools

William Boyd

Listen to this. Read it to yourself. Out Loud. Read it slow and think about it.

A swimming pool is like a child,
Leave it alone and it will surely run wild.

Who said that? Answer. Me. I did.

WINTERING

'Can I swim?' says Noelle-Joy. 'It's a fantastic pool.'

Much as I would like to see her jugs in a swimsuit I have to say no.

'Aw. Pretty please? Why not?'

'I'm afraid the pool is wintering.'

Noelle-Joy squints sceptically up at the clear blue sky. There's not even any smog today. She exposes the palms of her hands to the sun's powerful rays.

'But it's *hot*, man. Anyways, we don't get no winter in LA,' she argues.

Patiently I explain that, four seasons or no, every pool has to winter. A period of rest. What you might call a pool-sabbath. I've lowered the water level below the skimmers, superchlorinated, and washed out my cartridge filter. A pool, as I explain several times a day to my clients, is not just a hole in the ground filled with water. Wintering removes constant wear and tear, rests the incessantly churning pump machinery, allows essential repairs and maintenance, permits cleansing of the canals, filter system and heating units. You can't do all that if you're splashing around in the goddam thing. Most people realize I'm talking sense

We walk around my pool. It's small but it's got every-thing. No-Skid surrounds, terrace lights, skimmers, springboard, all-weather poolside furniture, and a bamboo cocktail bar plus hibachi. I've got to admit it looks kind of peculiar stuck in my little back yard. (In this part of the city it's the only private pool for seventeen blocks.) But so what! I busted my balls for that little baby. I got me a new vacuum sweep last month. I'm aiming for a sand filter now, to replace my old cartridge model.

I stand proudly behind the bar and pour Noelle-Joy a drink. She's wearing a yellow halter neck and tight purple shorts. Maybe if she was a little thinner they'd look a bit better on her . . . I don't know. If you got it, flaunt it, I guess. Her legs are kind of short and her thighs have got that strange rumpled look. She stacks her red hair high on top of her head to compensate. She lights a Kool, sips her drink, sighs and hugs herself. Then she sees my hibachi and screams. I drop my cocktail shaker.

'My God! A hibachi. Permanent as well. Hey, can we bar-b-q? Please? Don't tell me that's wintering too.'

I ignore her sarcasm. 'Sure,' I say, picking up ice cubes. 'Come by tomorrow.'

I work for AA1 Pools (Maintenance) Inc. We've also been ABC Pools and Aardvark Pools. I tell my boss Sol Yorty that we should call ourselves something like Azure Dreams, Paradise Pools, Still Waters – that kind of name. Yorty laughs and says it's better to be at the head of the line in Yellow Pages than sitting on our butts, poor, with some wise-ass, no-account trademark. The man has no pride in his work. If I wasn't up to my ears in hock to him I'd quit and set up on my own. TROPICAL LAGOONS, BLUE DIAMOND POOLS . . . I haven't settled on a name yet. The name is important.

GREEN WATER

Down Glendale Boulevard, Hollywood Freeway, on to Santa Monica Freeway. Got the ocean coming up. Left into Brentwood. Client lives off Mandeville Canyon. My God, the houses in Brentwood. The *pools* in Brentwood. You've never seen swimming pools like them. All sizes, all shapes, all eras. But nobody looks after them. I tell you, if pools were animate, Brentwood would be a national scandal.

The old Dodge van stalls on the turn up into the driveway. Yorty's got to get a new van soon, for Christ's sake. I leave it there.

The house stands at the top of a green ramp of lawn behind a thick laurel hedge. It's a big house, Spanish colonial revival style with half timbered English Tudor extension. A hispanic manservant takes me down to the pool. 'You wait here,' he says. Greaser. I don't like his tone. One thing I've noticed about this job, people think a pool cleaner is lower than a snake's belly. They look right through you. I was cleaning a pool up on Palos Verdes once. This couple started balling right in front of me. No kidding.

The pool. Thirty yards by fifteen. Grecian pillared pool house and changing rooms. Marble topped bar. Planted round with oleanders. I feel the usual sob build up in my throat. It's quiet. There's a small breeze blowing. I dip my hand in the water and shake it around some. The sun starts dancing on the ripples, wobbling lozenges of light, wavy chicken-wire shadows on the blue tiles. What is it about swimming pools? Just sit beside one, with a cold beer in your hand and you feel happy. It's like some kind of mesmeric influence. A trance. I said to Yorty once, 'Give everybody their own pool to sit beside and there'd be no more trouble in this world.' The fat moron practically bust a gut.

I myself think it's something to do with the colour of the water. That blue. I always say that they should call that blue 'swimming pool blue'. Try it on your friends. Say 'swimming pool blue' to them. They know what you mean right off. It's a special colour. The colour of tranquility. Got it! TRANQUILITY POOLS . . . Yeah, that's it. Fuck Yorty.

But the only trouble with this particular pool is it's *green*. The man's got green water.

'Hey,' I hear a voice. 'You come for the pools?'

I'm only wearing overalls with AA1 POOLS written across the back in red letters. This guy's real sharp. He comes down the steps from the house, his joint just about covered with a minute black satin triangle. He's swinging a bullworker in one hand. Yeah, he's big. Shoulders like medicine balls, bulging overhang of pectorals. His chest is shiny and completely hairless with tiny brown nipples, almost a yard apart. But his eyes are set close together. I guess he's been using the bullworker on his brain too. I've seen him on the TV. Biff Ruggiero, ex pro-football star.

'Mr Ruggiero?'

'Yeah, that's me. What's wrong wit da pool?'

'You got green water. Your filtration's gone for sure. You got a build up of algae. When was the last time you had things checked out?'

He ignored my question. 'Green water? Shit, I got friends coming to stay tomorrow. Can you fix it?'

'Can you brush your teeth? Sure I can fix it. But you'd better not plan on swimming for a week.'

. . . and this stupid asshole, Biff Ruggiero – you know, pro-footballer? – he hangs around all day asking dumb questions. 'Whatcha need all dat acid for?' So there I am, I'm washing out his friggin cartridges with phosphate trisoda and all this crap's like coming out. 'Holy Jesus,' says Mr Nobel prize-winner, 'where's all dat shit come from?' 'Jesus,' I laugh quietly to myself, 'he's so dumb he thinks Fucking is a city in China.'

I watch Noelle-Joy get out of bed. She stands for a while rubbing her temples.

'I'm going to take a shower,' she says.

I follow her through to the bathroom.

'It just shows you,' I shout over the noise of the water. 'Those cartridge filters may be cheap but they can be a real pain in the nuts. I told him to put in a sand filter like the one I'm getting. Six-way valve, automatic rinsage – '

Noelle-Joy bursts out of the cabinet, her little stacked body all pink from the shower. She heads back into the bedroom, towels off and starts to dress.

'Hey, baby,' I say. 'Listen. I thought of a great name. Tranquility pools.' I block out the letters in the air. 'Trang. Quil. It. Tee. Tranquility pools. What do you think?'

'Look,' she says, her gaze flinging around the room. 'Ah. I gotta, um, do some shopping. I'll catch up with you later, OK?'

Noelle-Joy moves in. Boy, dames sure own a lot of garbage. She works as a stapler in a luggage factory. We get on fine. But already she's bugging me to get a car. She doesn't like to be seen in the Dodge van. She's a sweet girl, but there are only two things Noelle-Joy thinks about. Money, and more money. She says I should ask Yorty for a raise. I say how am I going to do that seeing I'm already into him for a $5,000 sand filter. She says she wouldn't give the steam off her shit for a sand filter. She's a strong-minded woman but her heart's in the right place. She loves the pool.

'You look after this pool great, you know,' Ruggiero says. I'm de-ringing the sides with an acid wash. We cleaned up the green water weeks ago but we've got a regular maintenance contract with him now.

'I never realized, like, they was so complicated.'

I shoot him my rhyme.

'That's good,' Ruggiero says, scratching his chin. 'Say, you wanna work for me, full time?'

I tell him about my plans. Tranquility pools, the new sand filter, Noelle-Joy.

I come home early. An old lady called up from out on Pacific Palisades. She said her dog had fallen into her pool in the night. She said she was too upset to touch it, I had to fish it out with the long-handled pool sieve. It was one of those tiny hairy dogs. It had sunk to the bottom. I dragged it out and threw it in the garbage can.

'No poolside light, lady,' I said. 'You don't light the way, no wonder your dog fell in. If that'd got sucked into the skimmers you'd have scarfed up your entire filter system. Bust valves, who knows?'

Wow, did she take a giant shit on me. Called Yorty, the works. I had to get the mutt's body out of the trash can, wah it, lay it out on a cushion . . . No wonder I'm red-assed when I get home.

Noelle-Joy's out by the pool working on her tan. Fruit punch, shades, orange bikini, pushed-up breasts. There's a big puddle of water underneath the sunlounger.

'Hi, honey,' she calls, stretching. 'This is the life, yeah?'

I go mad. 'You been in the water?' I yell.

'What? . . . Yeah. So I had a little swim. So big deal.'

'How many times I got to tell you. The pool's wintering.'

'The pools been wintering for *three fucking months*!' she screams.

But I'm not listening, I run into the pool house. Switch on the filters to full power. I grab three pellets of chlorine – no, four – and throw them in. Then I get the sack of soda-ash, tip in a couple of spadefuls, just to be sure.

I stand at the pool edge panting.

'What do you think you're doing?' she accuses.

'Superchlorination,' I say. 'You swam in stagnant water. Who knows what you could of brought in.'

Now she goes mad. She stomps up to me. 'I just *swam* in your fucking pool, turd-bird! I didn't piss in it or nothing!'

I've got her there. 'I know you didn't,' I yell in triumph. 'Cause I can tell. I got me a secret chemical in that water. *Secret*. Anybody pisses in my pool it turns *black*!'

We made up of course. 'A lovers' tiff' is the expression I believe. I explain why I was so fired up. Noelle-Joy is all quiet and thoughtful for an hour or two. Then she asks me a favour. Can she have a housewarming party for all her friends? There's no way I can refuse. I say yes. We are real close that night.

OTO

OTO. I don't know how we ever got by without OTO, or orthotolodine, to give its full name. We use it in the Aquality Duo Test. That's how we check the correct levels of chlorination and acidity (pH) in a pool. If you don't get it right you'd be safer swimming in a cess pit.

I'm doing an OTO test for Ruggiero. He's standing there crushing a tennis ball in each hand. His pool is looking beautiful. He's got some guests around it – lean, tanned people. Red umbrellas above the tables. Rock music playing from the speakers. Light from the water winking at you. That chlorine smell. That fresh coolness you get around pools.

One thing I will say for Ruggiero, he doesn't treat me like some sidewalk steamer. And the man seems to be interested in what's going on.

I show him the two little test tubes lined up against the colour scales.

'Like I said, Mr Ruggiero, it's perfect. OTO never lets you down. You always know how your pool's feeling.'

'Hell,' Ruggiero says, 'looks like you got to be a chemist to run a pool. Am I right or am I right?' he laughs at his joke.

I smile politely and step back from the pool edge, watch the water dance.

'A thing of beauty, Mr Ruggiero, is a joy forever. Know who said that? An English poet. I don't need to run no OTO test. I been around pools so long I got an instinct about them. I know how they feel. Little too much acid, bit of algae, wrong chlorine levels . . . I see them, Mr Ruggiero, and they tell me.'

'Come on,' Ruggiero says, a big smile on his face. 'Let me buy you a drink.'

* * *

Sol Yorty looks like an ageing country and western star. He's bald on top but he's let his grey hair grow over his ears. He lives in dead end East Hollywood. I walk down the path in his back gareden with him. Yorty's carrying a bag of charcoal briquettes. His fat gut stretches his lime-green sports shirt skin tight. He and his wife Dolores are the fattest people I know. Between them they weigh as much as a small car. The funny thing about Yorty is that even though he owns a pool company he doesn't own a pool.

He tips the briquettes into his bar-b-q as I explain that I'm going to have to hold back on the sand filter for a month or two. This party of Noelle-Joy is going to make it hard for me to meet the deposit.

'No problem,' Yorty says. 'Glad to see you're making a home at last. She's a . . . She seems like a fine girl.' He lays out four huge steaks on the grill.

'Oh sorry, Sol,' I say. 'I didn't know you had company. I wouldn't have disturbed you.'

'Nah,' he says. 'Just me and Dolores.' He looks up as Dolores waddles down the garden in a pair of flaming orange bermudas and the biggest bikini top I've ever seen.

'Hey sweetie,' he shouts. 'Look who's here.'

Dolores carries a plastic bucket full of rice salad. 'Well hi, stranger. Wanna eat lunch with us? There's plenty more in the fridge.'

I say I've got to get back.

It looks like Noelle-Joy's invited just about the entire workforce from the luggage factory. Mainly guys too, a few blacks and hispanics. The house is crammed with guests. You can't move in the yard. This morning I vacuum-swept the pool, topped up the water level, got the filters going well, and threw in an extra pellet of chlorine.

You can't be too sure. Some of Noelle-Joy's friends don't seem too concerned about personal hygiene. Everybody, though, is being real nice to me. Noelle-Joy and I stand at the door greeting the guests. Noelle-Joy makes the introductions. Everyone smiles broadly and we shake hands.

I feel on edge as the first guests dive into the pool. I watch the water slosh over the sides, darkening the No-Skid surrounds. I hear the skimmer valves clacking madly.

Noelle-Joy squeezes my hand. She's been very affectionate these last few days. Now every few minutes she comes on over from talking to her friends and asks me if I'm feeling fine. She keeps smiling and looking at me. But it's what I call her lemon smile – like she's only smiling with her lips. Maybe she's nervous too, I think, wondering what her friends from the luggage factory will make of me.

I have to say I'm not too disappointed though, when I'm called away by the phone. It's from Mr Ruggiero's house. Something's gone wrong, there's some sort of sediment in the water. I think fast. I say it could be a precipitation of calcium salts and I'll be there right away.

I clap my hands for silence at the poolside. Everyone stops talking.

'I'm sorry folks,' I say, 'I have to leave you for a while. I got an emergency on. You all keep right on having a good time. I'll be back as soon as I can. Bye now.'

Traffic's heavy at this time of the day. We've got a gridlock at Western Avenue and Sunset. I detour round on the Ventura Freeway, out down through Beverly Glen, back on to Sunset and on in to Brentwood.

I run down the back lawn to the pool. I can see Ruggiero and some of his friends splashing around in the water. Stupid fools. The hispanic manservant tries to stop me but I just lower my shoulder and bulldoze through him.

'Hey!' I shout. 'Get the fuck out of that water! Don't you know it's dangerous? Get out, everybody, get out!'

Ruggiero's muscles launch him out of the pool like a dolphin.

'What's goin' on?' He looks angry and puzzled. 'You ain't a million laughs you know, man.'

I'm on my knees peering at the water. The other guests have clambered out and are looking around nervously. They think of plagues and pollution.

In front of my nose the perfect translucent water bobs and shimmies, nets of light wink and flash in my eyes.

'The sediment,' I say. 'The calcium salts . . . didn't somebody phone . . .?'

By the time I get back I've been away for nearly an hour and a half. She worked fast, I have to admit. Cleaned out everything. She and her friends, they had it all planned. I'd been deep-sixed for sure.

There was a note. YOU MAY NO A LOT A BOUT POOLS BUT YOU DONT NO SHIT A BOUT PEPLE.

I don't want to go out to the yard but I know I have to. I walk through the empty house like I'm walking knee deep in wax. The yard is empty. I can see they threw everything in the pool – the loungers, the tables, the bamboo cocktail bar, bobbing around like the remains from a shipwreck. Then all of them standing in a circle round the side, laughing, having their joke.

I walk slowly up to the edge and look down. I can see my reflection. The water's like black coffee.

Yorba Linda. It's just off the Riverside Expressway. I'm working as a cleaner at the public swimming pool. Open air, Olympic sized.

Yorty had to fire me after what he heard from Ruggiero.

Sol said he had no choice, he was sorry but he would 'have to let me go'.

I sold up and moved out after the party. That pool could never be the same after what they had done in it. I don't know – it had lost its innocence, I guess.

Funny thing happened. I was standing on Sunset and a van halted at an intersection. It was a Ford, I think. It was blue. I didn't get a look at the driver, but on the side, in white letters, was TRANQUILITY POOLS. The van drove off before I could get to it. I'm going to file a complaint. Somebody's stolen my name.

Greater Love

Iain Crichton Smith

He wore a ghostly white moustache and looked like a major in the First World War, which is exactly what he had been On our way to school – he being close to retiring age – he would tell me stories about the First World War and the Second World War, for he had been in both. As we were passing the chemist's shop he would be describing Passchaendale, walking along stiff and erect, his eyes glittering behind his glasses.

'And there I was crouched in this trench, with my water bottle empty. I had somehow or another survived. All my good boys were dead, some up to their chests in mud. The Jerries had got hold of our plan of attack, you see. What was I to do? I had to wait all night, that was clear. When the sun was just going down, I crawled along the trench, and then across No Man's Land. I met a Jerry and the struggle was fast and furious. I am afraid I had to use the bayonet, or cold steel as we called it. But the worst was not over yet, for one of our own sentries fired on me. But I eventually managed to give him the password. After that I was all right.'

He would pause and then as we passed the ironmonger's he would start on another story. He taught chemistry in the school and instead of telling his pupils about solutions, or whatever they do in chemistry, he would spend his time, talking about the Somme or the Marne. He spoke more about the First World War than he did about the Second.

Once at the school party there was a quarrel between him and the head of the French Department, who had also been in the First World War and who believed that he had won it. He questioned a statement which Morrison had made. It was, I think, a question of a date and they grew more and more angry and wouldn't speak to each other after that for a year or more. As I quite like both of them, it was difficult to know whose side to take.

The Headmaster didn't know what to do with him for parents came to the school continually to complain about his lessons – which as I have said consisted almost exclusively of accounts of his adventures in France and Flanders. The extraordinary thing was that he never repeated a story: all his tales were realistic and detailed and one could almost believe that they had happened to him. Either they had been experienced by him or they formed part of a huge mythology of legends which he had memorized, but which belonged to others. I was then Deputy Head of the school and it was my duty to see the parents and listen to their complaints.

'He will soon be retiring,' I would tell them soothingly. 'And he has been a good teacher in his time.'

And they would answer, 'That's all very well, but our children's education is being ruined. When are you going to speak to him?'

I did in fact try to speak to him a few times, but before I could do that he was telling me another of his stories and I found somehow or another that there was no way in which I could introduce my complaint to him.

'There was an angel, you know, at Mons, and I saw it. It was early morning and we were going over the top and we saw this figure bending over us from the sky. I thought it must have been an effect of the sun but it wasn't that. It was as if it was blessing us. We had our bayonets out and the light was flashing from them. I was in charge of a company at the time, the Colonel having been killed.'

This time I was so interested I said to him, 'Are you sure that it was an angel? After all, the rays of the sun streaming down . . . and you, I presume, being in an excited frame of mind . . .'

'No,' he said, 'it wasn't that . . . It was definitely an angel. I am quite sure of that. I could actually see its eyes.' And he turned to me. 'They were so compassionate. You have no idea what they looked like. You would never forget them.'

In those days we had lines and the pupils would assemble in the quadrangle in front of the main door and Morrison loved the little military drill so much that we gave him the duty most of the time. He would make them dress, keeping two paces between the files, and they would march into the school in an orderly manner.

A young bearded teacher called Cummings who was always bringing educatioal books into the staffroom didn't like this militarism at all. One day he said to me, 'He's teaching them to be soldiers. He should be stopped.'

'How old are you?' I asked him.

'Twenty-two. What's that to do with it?'

'Twenty-two?' I said. 'Run along and teach your pupils English.' He didn't like it but I didn't want to explain to him why his age was important: he wouldn't have understood in any case. Still I couldn't find a way of speaking to Morrison without offending him.

'You'll just have to come straight out with it,' my wife said.

'No,' I said.

'What else can you do?'

'I don't know,' I said.

I was very conscious of the fact that I was considerably

younger than Morrison. One day I said to him, 'How do you see your pupils?'

'What do you mean?'

'How do you see them?' I repeated.

'See them?' he said. 'They are too young to fight. But I see them as ready for it. Soon they will be taken.'

'Taken?'

'Yes,' he said. 'Just as we were taken.'

After a silence he said, 'One or two of them would make good officers. It's the gas that's the worst.'

'Have you told them about the gas?' I said, seizing on a tenuous connection between the First World War and chemistry.

'No,' he said, 'it was horrifying.'

'Well,' I said. 'Explain to them about the gas. Why don't you do that?'

'We never used it,' he said. 'The Jerries tried to use it, but the wind blew it back against them.' However, he promised that he would explain about the gas. I was happy that I had found a method of getting him to teach something of his subject, and tried to think of other connections. But I couldn't think of any more.

One day he came to see me, and said, 'A parent called on me today.'

'Called on you!' I said angrily. 'He should have come through me.'

'I know,' he said. 'He came directly to me. He complained that I was an inefficient teacher. Do you think I'm an inefficient teacher?'

'No,' I said.

'I have to warn them, you see,' he said earnestly. 'But I suppose I had better teach them chemistry after all.'

From that time onwards he became more and more melancholy and lost-looking.

He drifted through the corridors with his white ghostly moustache as if he was looking for a battle to take part in. Then he stopped coming to the staffroom and stayed in his classroom all the time. There were another three months to go before his retirement and if he carried on in this way I knew that he would fade away and die. Parents ceased to come and see me about him and I was worried.

One day I called the best chemistry student in the school – Harrison – to my room and said, 'How is Mr Morrison these days?'

Harrison paused for a moment and then he said, 'He's very absent-minded, sir.' We looked at each other meaningfully, he tall and handsome in his blue uniform with the blue braid at the cuffs of his jacket. I fancied for a moment that I saw a ghostly white moustache flowering at his lips.

'I see,' I said, fiddling with a pen which was lying on top of the red blotting paper which in turn was stained with drops of ink like flak. 'How are you managing, the members of the class I mean?'

'We'll be all right,' said Harrison. Though nothing had been said between us he knew what I was talking about.

'I'll leave you to deal with it then,' I said.

The following day Morrison came gleefully to see me. 'An extraordinary thing happened to me,' he said. 'Do you know that boy Harrison? He is very brilliant of course and will go on to university. He asked me about the First World War. He was very interested. I think he will make a good officer.'

'Oh,' I said.

'He has a fine mind. His questions were very searching.'

'I see,' I said, doodling furiously.

'I cannot disguise the fact that I was unhappy here for a while. I was thinking: here they are and I am unable to warn them of what is going to happen to them. You see, no one told us that there were going to be two world wars. I was in the sixth year when the First World War broke out. I was studying chemistry just like Harrison. They told us we would be home for Christmas. Then after I came back from the war I did chemistry in university. I forgot about the war and then the second one came along. By that time I was teaching here, as you know.'

'Yes,' I said.

'In the First World War I was so young. Everyone was so ignorant and naïve. No one told us anything. We were very enthusiastic, you see. You recollect of course that there hadn't really been a big war since the Napoleonic Wars. Naturally there had been the Boer War and the Crimean War, but these had been side issues.'

'Of course,' I said.

'You were in the Second World War yourself,' he said. 'So you will know.'

But as I had been in the Air Force that didn't in his opinion count. And yet I too had seen scarves of flame like those of students streaming from planes as they exploded in the sky. I felt the responsibility of my job intensely, and though I was younger I felt the older of the two. I felt protective towards him as if it was I who was the officer and he the young starry-eyed recruit.

After Harrison had asked him his questions Morrison was quite happy again to return to the First World War with a clear conscience. Then one day a parent came to see me. It was in fact Major Beith, a red-faced man with a fierce bristling moustache who had been an officer in the Second World War.

'What the bloody hell is going on?' he asked me. 'My son isn't learning any chemistry. Have you seen his report card? It's bloody awful.'

'He doesn't work,' I said firmly.

'I'm not saying that he's the best worker in the world. The bugger watches TV all the time. But that's not the whole explanation. He's not being taught. He got fifteen per cent for his chemistry.'

I was silent for a while and then I said, 'Education is a very strange thing.'

'What?' And he glared at me from below his bushy eyebrows.

I leaned towards him and said, 'What do you think education consists of?'

'Consists of? I send my son to the school to be taught. That's what education consists of. But the little bugger tells me that all he learns about is the Battle of the Marne.'

'Yes,' I said. 'I appreciate that. But on the other hand I sometimes think that . . .' I paused. 'He sees them, I don't know how he sees them. He sees them as the Flowers of Flanders. Can you believe that?'

His bulbous eyes raked me as if with machine gunfire.

'I don't know what you're talking about.'

I sighed. 'Perhaps not. He sees them as potential officers, and NCOs and privates. He is trying to warn them. He is trying to tell them what it is like. He loves them, you see,' I said simply.

'Loves them?'

'That's right. He is their commanding officer. He is preparing them.' And then I said daringly, 'What's chemistry in comparison with that?'

He looked at me in amazement. 'Do you know,' he said, 'that I am on the Education Committee?'

'Yes,' I said staring him full in the eye.

'And you're supposed to be in charge of discipline here?'

'I am,' I said. 'I have to think of everything. Teachers have rights too.'

'What do you mean, teachers have rights.'

'Exactly what I said. If pupils have rights so too have teachers. And one cannot legislate for love. He loves them more than you or I are capable of loving. He sees the horror waiting for them. To him chemistry is irrelevant.'

For the first time I saw a gleam of understanding passing across the cloudless sky of his eyes. About to get up, he sat down again, smoothing his kilt.

'It's an unusual situation,' I said, 'and by the nature of things it will not last long. The fact is that we don't know the horrors in that man's mind. Every day he is there he sees the class being charged by bayonets. He sees Germans in grey helmets. He smells the gas seeping into the room. He is protecting them. All he has to save them is his stories.'

'You think?' he said, looking at me shrewdly.

'I do,' I said.

'I see,' he said, in his crisp military manner.

'He is not like us,' I said. 'He is being destroyed by his imagination.' As a matter of fact I knew that the major's son was lazy and difficult and that part of the reason for that was the affair that his father was conducting with a married woman from the same village.

He thought for a while and then he said, 'He has only two or three months to go. We can last it out.'

'I knew you would understand,' I said.

He shook his head in a puzzled manner and then he left the room.

The day before he was to retire Morrison came to see me. 'They are as prepared as I can make them,' he said. 'There is nothing more I can do for them.'

'You've done very well,' I said.

'I have tried my best,' he said. 'Question and answer,' he said. 'I should have done it in that way from the beginning. Start from the known and work out to the unknown. But they didn't know enough so I had to start with the unknown.'

'There was no other way,' I said.

'Thank you,' he said courteously. And he leaned across the desk and shook me by the hand.

I said that I hoped he would enjoy his retirement, but he didn't answer.

'Goodbye for the present,' I said. 'I'm afraid I shall have to be away tomorrow. A meeting, you understand.' His eyes clouded for a moment and then he said, 'Well, goodbye then.'

I thought for one terrible moment that he would salute me, but he didn't. As a matter of fact I didn't see him often after his retirement. It was time that chemistry was taught properly. Later, however, I heard that he had lost his memory and couldn't tell his stories of the First World War any more. I felt this as an icy bouquet on my tongue, but the slate had to be cleaned, education had to begin again.

Biographical Notes

Scoular Anderson was born in 1946 and brought up in Argyll. He studied at Glasgow School of Art, then worked in London for seven years as an illustrator. He now lives in Glasgow, teaching art, illustrating books, painting and writing.

William Boyd was born in Accra, Ghana, in 1952. He was educated at Gordonstoun School and the universities of Glasgow and Oxford. He has written two novels: *A Good Man in Africa* (winner of the 1982 Somerset Maugham Award); *An Ice-Cream War* (nominated for the 1982 Booker Prize) and a collection of short stories, *On the Yankee Station*. His third novel *Stars and Bars* will be published in the autumn of 1984.

George Mackay Brown has always lived in Orkney. He has published five books of poems, two novels, four short story collections, three books for young people (legends and stories), four books on Orkney, and a play. He has numerous literary projects in varying stages of completion.

Ron Butlin was born in Edinburgh, where he now lives and works. He has published two collections of poetry, *Creatures Tamed by Cruelty* (Edinburgh University S.P.B., 1979) and *The Exquisite Instrument* (Salamander

Press, 1982). His short story collection *The Tilting Room* was published by Canongate in 1983.

Peter Chaloner is a Glaswegian solicitor in his thirties, now working as a paralegal in Philadelphia, USA. He studies Buddhism under Chogyam Trungpa, Rinpoche, and American law under the professors of Rutgers Law School, New Jersey. He also edits the Philadelphia literary magazine *Heat*. This is his fourth contribution to *Scottish Short Stories*.

Deirdre Chapman was born in Carnoustie, Angus, and now lives in Glasgow with her husband and three sons. She has worked for various newspapers in Glasgow and briefly in London, and has published a few short stories.

Elspeth Davie was born in Ayrshire and went to school in Edinburgh, studied at university and art college and taught painting for several years. She lived for a while in Ireland before returning to Scotland. She has published three novels: *Providings, Creating a Scene, Climbers on a Stair*, and three collections of short stories: *The Spark, The High Tide Talker, The Night of the Funny Hats*. She received Arts Council Awards in 1971 and 1977 and the Katherine Mansfield Short Story Prize in 1978. She is married and has one daughter.

Giles Gordon was brought up in Edinburgh but now lives in London with his wife and three children. He works as a literary agent, edits *Drama* quarterly and is *The Spectator*'s theatre critic. He is addicted to the short story, has published three of his own collections (as well as half a dozen novels) and edited various anthologies including *Modern Scottish Short Stories* (with Fred Urquhart)

(Faber); *Shakespeare Stories* (Hamish Hamilton); and *Modern Short Stories 1940–1980* (Everyman).

Alasdair Gray was born in Glasgow in 1934. Since leaving Glasgow art school in 1957 he has lived mainly by painting and writing. *The Origin of the Axletree* has recently appeared in the author's own anthology *Unlikely Stories Mostly* to be published in paperback by Penguin Books in 1984.

Robin Jenkins was born in Lanarkshire in 1912. He lives in Argyll, with long periods abroad. He has published nineteen novels and one volume of short stories.

James Kelman lives in Glasgow. His first full collection of short stories appeared in 1983 under the title *Not not while the giro* (Polygon Press, Edinburgh). Early in 1984 his first novel appeared. Entitled *The Busconductor Hines*, it is published by the same firm.

Bernard MacLaverty was born in Belfast in 1942. He is married with four children. He lives on the Isle of Islay and has recently given up teaching to write full time. He has published two collections of stories, *Secrets* and *A Time to Dance* and two novels, *Lamb* and *Cal*.

Brian McCabe was born in 1951 in Edinburgh, where he now lives. He has published two collections of poems, and his poems and short stories have appeared in various periodicals and anthologies and have been broadcast on the radio including *Firebird 1*. He was awarded a Writers Bursary by the Scottish Arts Council in 1980. He has done many public readings of his work and has recently given a number of readings and lectures in schools.

Iain Crichton Smith was born on the island of Lewis in 1928. He is a full-time writer, working in both Gaelic and English, and he has published novels, collections of short stories, poems and plays in both languages. His most recent publications in English are: *In the Middle* and *Selected Poems*; *The Hermit and Other Stories*; and *A Field Full of Folk*. His most recent Gaelic work is *An t-Aonaran*. He is married.

Alan Spence is in his mid-thirties and was born and raised in Glasgow. He has published a collection of short stories, *Its Colours They Are Fine* (1977), and two books of poems, *ah!* (1975) and *Glasgow Zen* (1981). He has also had plays broadcast on television and performed on stage. He is completing a novel, *The Magic Flute*, and another collection of stories, *Sailmaker*. He and his wife run the Sri Chinmoy Meditation Centre in Edinburgh.

Eric Woolston was born in Grimsby and educated in Chester. He spent the first decade of his working life in a variety of jobs in London and for the past decade has been a lecturer in Glasgow. He is married with two daughters.